Mr. Hobbs' Vacation

MR.
HOBBS'
VACATION

by
EDWARD STREETER

drawings by
DOROTHEA WARREN FOX

HARPER & BROTHERS, NEW YORK

Library of Congress catalog card number: 54-6030

Contents

v

Mr. Hobbs' Vacation

Curtain up

The incoming tide nosed its way inquiringly into dozens of rock-rimmed coves and tiny inlets. It edged up the slopes of the deserted beaches, pushing before it a line of seaweed and the brittle remains of horeshoe crabs. The advance guard of its encroaching waters crowded boldly between the shore rocks, then, grown suddenly timid, rushed back to the protection of the sea.

Over the coves and along the edges of the beaches circled the sea gulls and the terns, weaving, swooping, driving against the wind with powerful wings, then sliding and slipping down its slopes like boys on a sled run, plummeting suddenly after a fish, missing, rising again to resume their graceful, endless routine.

This is what they had been doing when the first savages built their huts of mud and sticks behind these dunes. This is what they were doing when the sails of the white men first passed along these shores. This is probably what they would be doing when, in some far distant age, the Island would again be deserted by man.

To the gulls, circling and swooping just off the lonely beaches, the only evidences that man had not already decamped were the roofs of the summer cottages which were visible here and there above the dune grass. Even these would not have been convincing proof of habitation, however, as their windows and doors were sealed with weather-stained shutters and weeds grew in the paths and driveways that led to them.

Had a gull, more inquisitive than the others, however, taken an exploratory flight eastward to a place where the coastline bent back on itself like a great fishhook, its sharp eyes would have noted the village of Rock Harbor basking sleepily in the late May sunlight. Here the evidence of man's presence became unmistakable although a gull familiar with the district would be conscious, as it circled over the tree-shaded streets and twisting lanes, that the population had not yet completely emerged from its long winter hibernation.

Only a few people moved along the sidewalks, meeting, stopping for a moment and passing on. Only a few automobiles stood beside the high curbs of the main street. In the harbor only fishermen's skiffs swung lazily at their moorings and the masts of the pleasure boats were missing.

A closer observer, however—one more used to the ways of men than a sea gull—would have noted a certain quiet bustle pervading the town. Men on ladders were busily slapping white paint on the clapboards of ancient houses and the soft spring breeze carried the sound of hammers.

In front of the A & P, Allen Perkins was setting up two long bicycle racks on either side of the entrance. Further down the street Alexander Kniska, owner of the Starland Theatre, was moodily scraping an inch of accumulated handbills from his display boards and in the windows of Terrey's General Store, Elwell Terrey and Miss Haskell were arranging the new summer merchandise.

In front of the Town Hall, Clyde Peabody, Chief of Police, sat on a bench in the sun, shaking a collection of pebbles in the cup of his work-hardened hand. Mr. Peabody had a melancholy, patient face not unlike that of an underfed bloodhound. His friend Bartlett White, the cashier of the First National Bank of Rock Harbor, sat beside him scratching lines in the dust with a stick.

"Vincent says he got word from Judge Brock this morning to get the place open the tenth of June," observed Mr. Peabody.

"Yeah, an' I hear Mrs. Gabrielson and her mother are coming in that weekend. I guess they like to get here early to look the others over." Mr. White drew several circles with his stick. "They're earlier than last year though. I wonder has the Judge got that pack of grandchildren with him."

"Guess he has. Ain't nobody else in that bunch of crazy coots that's got enough money to take care of 'em."

"Crazy's what they are all right. They pay good though."

"Yeah, that's what everybody says. Must take all the Judge has got to keep up with that gang. Remember last season how that youngest grandson of his pretty near took the corner off Allen Avery's diner with the old man's station wagon?"

"Ought to. I was having lunch in it."

A truck rattled down the street, a half load of matched boarding crashing about in the rear. They both raised a hand in salutation.

"Guess Gus is going to fix up those bathhouses."

"They sure need it all right. I don't see why these summer people stand for 'em—an' *pay* to use 'em at that."

"People that'll go in water as cold as that'll stand for anything."

Mr. White rose. "Well, I got to be getting back to the bank," he said. His eye wandered down the deserted street. "Twon't be long now before that street'll be so full of automobiles an' bicycles a snake couldn't get through."

"You're telling *me*," said Mr. Peabody morosely. "I'm the one that's got to take it in the neck."

"That's right," said Mr. White, removing his hat to rub his thinning hair. "You're the one that's got to take it all right. I guess we all got to, more or less, though. It's a funny thing—you can't live with 'em an' you can't live without 'em."

"You said something, Bart."

"Well whether you can or can't you better get your iron-toed shoes fixed 'cause come this time next month, they'll be running over your feet three a minute. By the way, you and Emily want to play a little bridge tonight?"

"Sounds all right to me, Bart. I'll speak to her when I go home to dinner. I'll have her give Betty a ring." He watched the cashier gloomily as the latter walked down the street toward the harbor and the bank.

His thoughts were as gloomy as his face for he realized that the time was rapidly approaching when he would cease to be Clyde Peabody, respected citizen of Rock Harbor, and a member of the School Board, and would become merely the Chief of Police of a fashionable summer colony—a glorified Keystone Cop—a person to be run into by little girls on bicycles, kidded by fuzzy-chinned boys in Ford convertibles, bombarded by damnfool questions and frustrated by a continuous traffic snarl which no one but himself made any effort to unravel.

From the middle of each September to the middle of the following June, Mr. Peabody and his fellow townsmen led lives like those of millions of other citizens of the United States. They earned a slender, but sufficient living at their various occupations. Their wants were few and their pleasures simple —a first-class television set, the movies, an occasional committee meeting at the Town Hall or a church supper, a business trip to the Mainland now and then, and frequent games of after-dinner bridge.

Then on June 16, like a troupe of actors, they would don their various costumes and climb onto the stage for the annual three-months pageant. No longer would they be Citizens, but rather Characters, expected to act out their parts without a letdown, prancing about the stage to be stared at, laughed at, patronized and generally pushed around by a group of summer people who (quite unconsciously) would also be playing roles completely alien to their normal winter lives.

The only difference was that the "native" troupe was paid for its acting while the summer group paid handsomely for the privilege of being allowed to appear on the stage at all.

Chief Peabody arose, stretched and opened a door marked "Police Headquarters."

"Going to dinner, George," he said. "You take over."

"Okay, Clyde."

As the spring sun mounted higher it baked the tingle out of the clear air. There was a warmth to its rays which foretold the delights of days to come. Even the sea gulls sensed it and their swoops and glides more and more took on the aspect of an aerial ballet.

2

Sight unseen

Didn't that sign say Rock Harbor?" asked Mrs. Hobbs.

"I don't know," said Mr. Hobbs crossly. "How can anybody know where we are if you go past every sign sixty miles an hour?"

"I was sure it said Rock Harbor," said Mrs. Hobbs complacently, bringing the car slowly to a halt.

There was a violent disturbance among the cartons, suitcases and loose objects which completely filled the rear. "Well, let's get there, that's all I care," said a female voice. "I'm almost dead."

Mrs. Hobbs backed the car to the road sign. "There. Who's right?" she cried cheerily. "Rock Harbor. Six and a half miles." She swung the car down the road to the left.

"I do hope the place is as nice as Retta said it was going to be," she said after a short silence.

"It had better be," said Mr. Hobbs. "For what we're paying for it, it ought to be a castle. Fool idea anyway renting a house we've never seen in a place we've never been to."

"I'd feel just the way you do, dear, except Retta's got such heavenly taste. And then she warned us, you remember, that none of these seashore houses are *pretty*. That's why they're so quaint."

Mr. Hobbs grunted.

"And as for its being in a place we've never seen, that's what I like about it. Everyone ought to get out of the old ruts once in a while and try something new. Retta says if people would make more effort to broaden their horizons they wouldn't be running to psychiatrists all the time. And besides it isn't *really* a strange place, Rog. There are loads of Cleveland people here that we know and it's going to be a lot of fun seeing *them*."

"Why?" said Mr. Hobbs. "It isn't in Cleveland."

"Oh Rog, you know what I mean. It'll be fun doing things with people we know."

"How's that going to broaden my horizons?" asked Mr. Hobbs.

"Oh darling," said Mrs. Hobbs soothingly, as one dealing with a difficult child. "You're just tired and cross. Wait till you see—what's the name of the place?—"

"Grey Gables," said the voice in the rear. "Let's go."

"How stupid. Of course. Grey Gables. And you know the last thing Retta said was that it's far enough away from Rock

Harbor so we'll have privacy and near enough so we can join in things whenever we want. And that little Pirates' Cove right by the house—Retta says it just *makes* the place."

"Step on it or let me out," said the voice from the back seat.

"This must be it," said Mrs. Hobbs. "That real-estate man said follow this road for eight and six-tenths miles and Grey Gables would be the fourth house on the left after we passed the pond."

"I'm afraid you're right," said Mr. Hobbs.

A plump, freckled face, framed with disheveled yellow hair, emerged from the bundles and boxes in the rear of the car. It was the face of a cherub—a face which still reflected the merry innocence of youth, but also gave indications of a more earthy beauty in the offing.

"Good Lord, Pop. Don't tell me we're going to live out in *this* wilderness. I thought we came down here to have some *fun*."

It was a rambling, two-story, gray shingled house, surrounded on three sides by a deep porch which, in the fading light, gave the whole lower floor a cavernous look. Above the porch rose an amazing series of corner bays and gables, joined together by a complex system of scrollwork.

Its massive bulk stood in the middle of a treeless lawn in which the crab grass struggled for supremacy with the weeds. Along its edges, waiting to move in at the slightest encouragement, were acres of bay and huckleberry bushes.

In the rear of the house the lawn continued to the edge of what appeared to be a bluff and beyond that was the flat, gray sea. A dense fog was rolling in over the water. Its wings had already reached the land on either side so that Grey Gables appeared to be standing in the middle of a ghostly amphitheater. A pair of mewing gulls circled the house then dropped out of sight below the bluff.

"Did you ever see anything so ducky in your life!" cried Mrs. Hobbs.

Mr. Hobbs looked at her with an astonishment that time would never completely extinguish. "Ducky" was not the word he would have chosen to describe Grey Gables. To him it was more reminiscent of an abandoned hotel—long abandoned and for sinister reasons. Poe, he thought, must have had such a place in mind when he wrote "The Fall of the House of Usher." It was the kind of a place to which one might ask Mary Roberts Rinehart and Charles Addams for a weekend of writing and sketching.

Mrs. Hobbs gave a delighted squeal. "There's the Pirates' Cove. Look, Kate. You remember Aunt Retta telling us about it. Imagine the fun you can have there."

"Doing what?" asked Kate.

The fog suddenly blotted out the sea. Below them, to the right, Mr. Hobbs made out the blurred outlines of a sandy cove, protected at its outer edges by jagged rocks. "Everybody bring something," he said. "Don't just go off and leave everything to me." He was too late. Mrs. Hobbs and Kate had already disappeared into the house empty-handed.

The front door creaked. As far as Mr. Hobbs was concerned it was just what a front door should have done in a place like this. Had a bat flown past his ear he would not have been surprised.

Mrs. Hobbs' voice came to him out of the gloom.

"There's a project for you, darling. Your first project. Oiling the front door. My, you're going to have fun puttering around this dear old place."

Mr. Hobbs felt as if he was entering a vast tomb. He slapped at the walls on either side of the door. "I can't find the switch," he said to no one in particular.

Through the darkness he saw a round gray object, apparently suspended from the ceiling in the middle of the room. He stumbled toward it, half expecting that it would turn out to be a snake. It was an electric light bulb, dangling naked and unadorned from the end of a cord.

"I'll be damned," he muttered as he switched on the light.

"I know," said Mrs. Hobbs. "We're so lucky to have electricity. Retta says a lot of the houses further out have no conveniences at all."

Mr. Hobbs looked about him and shuddered slightly. He was in a large room, the walls and ceiling of which were lined with matched boarding, stained a dark brown and varnished. In the center was a table, littered with last year's magazines, its legs connected with some kind of basketwork. Scattered about were several armchairs, all from the same basket factory. They had a sprung look as if they had been frozen in the act of collapsing.

In a corner a pile of green wooden chairs had been nested, one into the other. A chintz-covered sofa, at one end of which some heavy body had created a kind of bucket seat, com-

pleted the furnishings unless one included a number of paint-
ings which gave evidence of having been the summer work
of a former tenant who hadn't dabbled much in paints up to
that time.

Mrs. Hobbs was struggling with a French door. Its bottom
appeared to be nailed to the floor. The top flailed back and
forth with shattering crashes. "It seems to be stuck," she said.
"It must be enchanting though when the sun's out."

Mr. Hobbs pushed open a swinging door in the back of
the living room. A stale odor of drains came forth to greet him
through the twilight. "This must be the kitchen," he said.
"When does Brenda get here?"

"Tomorrow," said Mrs. Hobbs. "You don't remember anything, dear. It's going to be such fun just to be by ourselves for
a day and have a chance to make everything cozy." Again Mr.
Hobbs looked at her with unbelieving eyes.

Kate was lying on the broken sofa. "I knew this was going
to be awful," she said. "But I didn't think it was going to be
as awful as *this*. What's anybody going to *do* in a place like
this?"

"Now, Kate, you just stop that. This is your father's vacation. He's come down here for a rest and relaxation. You'll
find plenty to do." Kate sniffed.

"There's no water," said Mr. Hobbs from the kitchen.

"Oh dear, don't you remember that real-estate man in
the village said there wouldn't be any pressure up, but
that he'd left directions on the mantelpiece for starting the
pump."

They found the folded paper. Mr. Hobbs took it over to one

of the basketwork chairs, turned on a standing lamp and sat down to read.

The pump is very simple and should start easy. Open the petcock on top of the cylinder. Pour in two teaspoonfulls of gasolene (white—don't use no red). Remove rear plug in head of pump and prime with pint of water. Shut off valve to pressure tanks. Open overflow valve. Adjust set screw clockwise 1½ turns. Press down hard on foot starter. If engine don't start first time keep on jamming down on foot starter then adjust set screw counterclockwise as engine warms. Open butterfly valve. Close overflow valve. Open valve to pressure tank. When pressure gauge reaches 50 lbs. turn off by pressing screwdriver against spark plug and engine head else you'll blow out the tank.

"I don't like to hurry you, dear," said Mrs. Hobbs, "but couldn't you read that tomorrow? I'd like to get that pump going as quickly as possible so we can get some hot water."

Mr. Hobbs turned the creased, worn paper over and over like a man in a daze. "Water," he said. "Hot water. I don't know what the hell this guy's talking about. I don't even know where the pump *is*. I couldn't see to do anything if I found it. I wouldn't know what to do if I could see. We'll use what's left in the thermos jug tonight. Tomorrow I'll get some bright young fellow from M.I.T. to come down and make a study of this thing."

"Roger Hobbs, do you mean we're not going to have any hot water tonight?"

"You're not going to have any *water*, period."

"But do you know what that means? We can't take baths. Why I've been looking forward to a hot bath for hours."

"Well, I've *got* to take one," said Kate defiantly. "So that's that."

"Okay with me, but I guess you'll have to take them out of tea cups," said Mr. Hobbs gloomily. He replaced the directions on the mantelpiece. "I think I'll see if I can find that bottle. It's somewhere in the back of the car."

"What bottle?" asked Mrs. Hobbs, but he was gone.

That night Mr. Hobbs lay very still in his narrow iron bed. He would have liked to toss and turn, but one might as well try to be restless in a sagging hammock. He dozed and then woke in a cold sweat dreaming that he had been thrown into a sack and was being carried away over someone's shoulder.

Outside a hazy moon was trying to pierce the fog. He thought of his comfortable bed at home, of his blue-tiled bathroom where the water leaped forth from the faucets at any desired temperature, of his comfortable library with its worn leather chair which fitted every curve of his body, of his little bar under the hall stairs with all the gadgets hanging neatly from their wooden pegs.

He thought of the hitherto unrealized comfort and convenience of his life in those already remote days and reached for a sleeping pill. His hand pawed the air. Of course—there was no bedside table. The sleeping pills lay out there somewhere in a welter of unseen suitcases. They might just as well be back in Cleveland.

He groaned slightly, hoping to attract Peggy's sympathy, but he knew from her even breathing that she was asleep. His groan was unexpectedly answered by the moan of a foghorn from somewhere in the night.

3

Where do we go from here?

The Fates like to amuse themselves by mixing up the private affairs of unrelated mortals. An excellent example of this type of meddling occurred several months prior to the events chronicled in the last chapter.

During the early spring, while the Islanders were taking inventory of their diminishing coal and oil supplies in the annual hope that they might be stretched out to meet the coming of warm weather, a series of conferences were being held in another part of the country, the results of which were to have a direct impact on many an unsuspecting Rock Harbor citizen.

Hundreds of miles away, in the region referred to as "The Middle West" by those living east of the Alleghenies and "The East" by those living west of the Mississippi, a family by the name of Hobbs wrestled grimly with the well-nigh un-solvable problem of selecting a place in which to spend Mr. Hobbs' vacation which would be satisfactory to all the members of his large family—and reasonably acceptable to him.

As a matter of fact Mr. Hobbs was the only one who did not take an active part in these debates. He knew from experience that the dice were loaded against him and in such situations he had learned that the most dignified thing to do was to sit apart and look slightly amused—an attitude which had the additional advantage of being unbearably irritating.

Left to his own devices, Mr. Hobbs might have chosen places which would have surprised even those who knew him best. Like many successful and outwardly hard-headed businessmen he was a romanticist at heart. But this was a weakness which he concealed as a bride conceals a false tooth.

Had the question been put to him he would have voted for vague, faraway places—places where the natives wore strange and colorful costumes, if any—and unscalable, snowclad peaks cast purple shadows over jungles and sand-swept deserts. Actually he was not very clear about where these places were, but it did not matter, for no one would have taken him seriously if he had been able to put his finger on them in the dark.

Mrs. Hobbs' idea of earthly bliss, on the other hand, was to reassemble her rapidly expanding, and even more rapidly dis-integrating, family. She declared that she was willing to go anywhere at all as long as her beloved children were around her. Actually she was a bit less than honest in this statement, for Mrs. Hobbs was what might be called grandchild-happy, and much as she loved her children she would have sacrificed them all with a whoop and committed mayhem to boot in order to get her hands on her three grandchildren for one precious month. Also "anywhere at all" was to Mrs. Hobbs a much more definite place than the phrase implied.

She had already visualized a big, rambling summer cottage somewhere on the New England coast—a place where the swimming was good, which to Mrs. Hobbs meant lying on the sand for hours in and out of the shade of a beach umbrella—a place where there would be young people for Kate—and a place where the grandchildren could roll around under her ever watchful and delighted eyes.

As for the three Hobbs girls, they had all reached the age when they definitely resented being forced to make plans. On the other hand they had not yet outgrown the belief that it was their prerogative to find the home nest ready and wait-ing, with the beds turned down, whenever the wings of free-dom grew weary.

To all Mrs. Hobbs' pleas for some indication of what their plans for the coming summer might be their answer was that it would be quite impossible for them to make up their minds so far ahead of time. Mr. and Mrs. Hobbs should not really count on them at all. That would be the safest thing. Then, if none of the nebulous and half-baked summer projects, which they now had in mind, should materialize, they would turn up at the last minute.

Kate, who, until recently, would have gone without question wherever her family chose to take her, was showing the influence of two years at Smith. She was going abroad, she said. It was not so much that she yearned for the cultural advantages of Europe, but rather because three of her closest friends were going and for Kate every other spot on the globe had thereby become a dump.

Mr. Hobbs said he didn't want to restrict Kate's horizons, but he just didn't have what it took to maintain a city home, a country home and send his daughter gallivanting all over the world. That sort of thing, he declared, was for racketeers who didn't pay their income taxes.

Kate said she didn't think a simple little trip to Europe was "gallivanting all over the world" and besides she was too old to be treated like a horse and vanned around by her parents from one premarital show to another. As for the cost she would pay *every cent,* and she meant *every cent,* out of her own money. All she asked was that Mr. Hobbs loan it to her to begin with and then take it out of her allowance beginning after she had paid some of her current bills.

Mrs. Hobbs' two married daughters were even more difficult and in view of the fact that the possession of the grandchildren hinged on them they were vital to her plans.

Both, unfortunately, lived out of town. For two months Mrs. Hobbs had been phoning and writing and pleading in a vain attempt to pin them down.

"Mother, we just can't *tell*." Jane Grant was standing in the midst of the chaos that was her living room. "Byron just never knows whether he's going to take a vacation or not. He may teach in summer school. He may work on his book. He may want to spend it with his mother. We may be in *Alaska*—"

"Alaska!" exclaimed Mrs. Hobbs with alarm.

"Well, you know, mother—*anywhere*. You can't *tell* where we might go. Why don't you and Dad just plan without us. You both ought to get off somewhere by yourselves and forget your family for a while."

Mrs. Hobbs knew that they would come at the last minute, but this sort of talk always made her panicky. "You know perfectly well, Jane, that your father wouldn't hear of such a thing. He just lives for those grandchildren. No, it simply means that we'll have to find some place big enough to take you all and then hope that someday you'll be able to make up your minds about *something*."

Susan wrote: "Mother, we just can't plan so far ahead. We may be with you, but you mustn't be disappointed if we only turn up for a day or two—or not at all. Stew hates to be pinned down. It makes him awfully nervous. You know how temperamental and sensitive he is. He's the kind that likes to wake up in the morning and say 'let's go' and then go."

Mrs. Hobbs sighed.

"I had lunch today with Retta Nickerson," said Mrs. Hobbs.

"Nothing unusual about that," said Mr. Hobbs. "If you *didn't* have lunch with Retta Nickerson *that* might be news.

Like that whaler's log in the New Bedford Museum. It only mentions the Captain's drinking habits once during a two-year cruise. Then it says, 'The Captain was not drunk today.' "

"What a silly thing to put in," said Mrs. Hobbs. "There's no point to it anyway because Retta and I never take a cocktail in the middle of the day. Now I can't remember what I started to tell you. I wish you wouldn't do that."

"You had lunch with Retta Nickerson," said Mr. Hobbs patiently.

"Oh yes. Well, you know the Nickersons always go to Rock Harbor for Jack's vacation."

Mr. Hobbs nodded vacantly. He was thinking of a man he had to see the next morning.

"Well, they're not going this year, but Retta says she knows a house that would be just right for us. It's big enough for the whole family and it's got a little beach of its own where the children could play."

"Rock Harbor's too rich for my blood," said Mr. Hobbs. "Besides I wouldn't want to go to that kind of a place anyway. Too much dressing up, and la de da—and all that sort of thing."

"Well, darling, that's exactly why Retta thought this house was made to order for us. It's *not* expensive because, from what Retta said, I guess it's not one of the *newest* houses. And then she said it was about eight miles outside Rock Harbor so that you could mix into things or not just as you felt like. So you see it would be fun for Kate, and heavenly for the grandchildren—and just what you want—"

"In what way?" asked Mr. Hobbs. But he knew the matter had been decided.

"It's called Grey Gables," said Mrs. Hobbs.

As the weeks passed and the winter softened into spring, Mr. Hobbs quietly began to dramatize Grey Gables. Little by little he built its low, gray walls, its spacious rooms with great picture windows looking out over the sea, its broad flagstone terrace protected from the wind by a rose-covered wall where one could lie in the sun and enjoy just being alive.

He couldn't lie long, however, even in his daydreams. Mr. Hobbs was a high-powered person who was in the habit of organizing situations as they came along.

There were the children and the grandchildren, for instance—a thousand and one things to be done with them. There were long evenings of talk when he would have an opportunity to know his two sons-in-law better. There were afternoon walks on lonely beaches, collecting shells, telling stories, revealing the beautiful world to eager, upturned faces. There were long, lazy days when one just lay on the warm sand listening to the break of the waves.

And then there were so many other things that he would like to do. He had always wanted to sail. That experience as a deckhand in the Bermuda races had whetted his appetite for the tang of salt sea spray in his face. He would rent a boat and race it with the kids. On days when there was no racing they would sail it to fascinating little islands where they would have picnic lunches followed by intimate, drowsy talks.

Nature. That was another thing he wanted to tackle. It

was stupid not to know the names of things. He'd buy a book. He saw himself lying on his stomach in the grass beside a meadow pond. Above and below the seemingly calm surface of the water he watched the savage fight of tiny creatures for their very existence. At his side was a notebook in which he occasionally jotted the name of an insect or a shrub. Above his head a flight of geese honked southward.

And then there was, of course, the ever-present matter of his body. Mr. Hobbs was conscious of the fact that he was no longer in the old pink, but he was still at the stage in life when he regarded this as a temporary condition which would be quickly corrected as soon as he had time to attend to it.

During the last four or five years he'd been so busy at the office that he had given little attention and practically no exercise to what he liked to refer to as the temple of his soul. As a result it had a tendency to shapelessness. For a month he would go into training, cut down on the intake and exercise methodically each day. He would come back in the fall looking like Victor Mature. He could hear the gasps of surprise as he strode down the street on the way to the office. "Roger, I hardly knew you. How in the world did you do it?"

Mr. Hobbs stood in front of the long mirror on the bathroom door, drew in his breath and sucked in his stomach in what was intended to be a preview of coming events. The result was not entirely satisfactory, but one could get the general idea.

4

It's a good little pump

The sun climbed out of the ocean and eventually worked itself up to the level of Mr. Hobbs' window sill. As its brassy rays shone in his face he opened his eyes, then closed them again quickly and pulled his head under the covers. He needed this seclusion to gather his wits, for he did not have the foggiest idea where he was—or how he came to be in a hammock. Gradually he realized that it was not a hammock, but a bed—a white iron bed with tired springs.

Raising himself cautiously he looked out over a deep blue sea sparkling in the golden morning light. From somewhere off shore came the muffled put-put of a lobsterman's dory. He suddenly felt a great urge to be outside, to be a part of this dazzling scene. Above all things he did not want to wake anyone. This particular moment belonged to him. Hobbs walks alone! The dawn patrol! He looked at his wrist watch. It was eight o'clock. Well anyway, he wanted to do it alone.

"Rog, won't you *please* get after that pump." Mrs. Hobbs was regarding him sleepily from the adjoining bed.

The sun lost its sparkle. The room became an ugly, matchboarded enclosure. He had forgotten all about the damn pump. He found a pair of slippers and a dressing gown in one of the suitcases, put them on and went to the window. There, to the right, was the Pirates' Cove. He could see a path descending to it through the bayberry bushes. Halfway down the slope was a little shack. That must be the pump.

He found a towel and went downstairs to reread the directions for starting the thing. The living room looked even uglier by daylight than it had the night before, but somehow less depressing. Once off by himself the sense of high adventure began to return. He slipped the directions into the pocket of his dressing gown and started down the path, humming a little tune.

"Tiny little thing," he murmured as he opened the door of the pumphouse. Such a midget of an engine ought to be easy. Carefully, step by step, he followed the instructions. It took time, but he thought he had them right. It gave him a feeling of self-confidence. Now a smart push down on the foot pedal and off we go.

He put his foot on the starter and jabbed it down with all his might. It smacked against the concrete floor with an ankle-jarring crash. The flywheel turned over stiffly. There was a sucking noise. Then all was still. But then the directions had given a hint that the thing might not start at the first kickover. On a crisp morning like this it might take two or three goes.

Half an hour later Mr. Hobbs had shed his bathrobe and the top of his pajamas. He rested his arm against the jamb of the pumphouse door and laid his head against it. He could feel the sweat trickling down his ribs and chest and the thumping of his heart must have been audible several feet away.

A flight of crows passed over, cawing excitedly, but that was the only sound. The little engine remained cold and silent. "This is it," he thought as his heart continued to hammer. "This is journey's end for Hobbs. 'Mr. Hobbs was found face down in the bushes where he had evidently lain for a long time.' And all so that a couple of women can get nice hot water for their baths. Bah!"

Forgetting that he was wearing slippers he kicked the engine. The pain enraged him. It was as if the engine had kicked him. He would start the damn thing or die in his tracks right here. Savagely he jumped up and down on the foot starter, his breath coming in coughing gasps.

He did not hear Mrs. Hobbs descending the path. She stopped behind him. "Isn't this too, too heavenly," she said. Her eyes went round the horizon and came to rest on his glistening back. "Are you having trouble with the pump, dear?" Her tone was that of one who wants to share in all that is going on around her in a beautiful world, even though some of it may be quite boring.

Mr. Hobbs stopped jumping on the foot starter. He replaced his pajama coat and dressing gown and recovered his bath towel from the top of the pumphouse door. "Yes," he said.

"Do you think there's something the matter with it, dear?"

"Yes," he said and walked silently down the path toward the cove. Mrs. Hobbs watched him anxiously. It seemed to her that he tottered just a wee bit.

"I do wish you'd get it started, dear," she called after him. "I have just enough water left for the coffee."

Mr. Maurio of the Rock Harbor Utilities and Real Estate Company did not seem in the least surprised to see Mr. Hobbs enter his office.

"Something wrong out at Grey Gables?" he inquired cheerfully.

Mr. Hobbs assured him that he was correct. Something was wrong, very wrong. There was not a drop of water in the damned house because the damned pump was no good. Busted. Caput. He had a houseful of people and he was damned—

Mr. Maurio listened attentively, nodding his head from time to time. "That's a good pump," he said finally. "Best kind of pump."

Mr. Hobbs gripped the edge of Mr. Maurio's desk. "I'm telling you," he said with restrained dignity, "that no matter how good it is it doesn't work."

"Won't start, you mean?" suggested Mr. Maurio.

"One hundred per cent correct," said Mr. Hobbs.

Mr. Maurio studied a large discolored real-estate map of Rock Harbor which almost covered the opposite wall. "Guess you'll have to get Fred Saltonstall to look it over. Sounds as if it may need a bit of adjusting."

"Who's Fred Saltonstall?"

"Plumber. Fine fellow. Takes care of all the summer people. You ought to get to know him right away."

"Where do I get hold of him?"

Mr. Maurio did some thoughtful doodling on a pad of paper. "That's hard to tell," he said finally. "He might be to home—and then he might not. He might be out on a job—and again he might be doing something else."

"What do you *think*? I've got to do something."

"Well, you might take a chance an' call his home, but then if he's not there you've wasted a call. Wife's there, perhaps. She's apt to know where he's gone. He's at 62-W3. I got to go out. You sit here and call him. May take you a little while. Party line."

Mr. Hobbs picked up the receiver. A high-pitched, female voice came over the wire. "She was over last night. She and Jim came over after supper. They brought the two children. I want to tell you, May, I've seen some brats, but I never seen anything to beat those two. You know that blue table cover—"

Mr. Hobbs replaced the receiver noiselessly on its cradle and picked up a copy of *The Real Estate Age*. After a few minutes he tried again.

"—an' I says to her, 'That may be all right for you. You were asked. But I wasn't and I don't go places I'm not asked.' I says, 'If Estelle Peterson thinks for one minute—' "

This time Mr. Hobbs replaced the receiver with a bang. Five minutes later he picked it up again. The female voice still droned on. He cleared his throat loudly. "Listen, May, there's somebody eavesdropping on this line. It's getting so's a body can't enjoy a minute's conversation without some big nose snooping around." There was a brief silence during which Mr. Hobbs thought he could detect the sound of indignant breathing. "I guess he's gone. Whoever it was he's no gentleman. Well as I was saying I took this sample into Elwell Terrey an' I says, 'Good morning, Elwell.' You know, May, I sometimes think that man has something the matter with him. He has those awful bags under his eyes—'specially in the morning. It might be kidneys. His mother had kidneys. You knew that, May, didn't you? I think she died of 'em. Let's see where was I?—"

"Nowhere," shouted Mr. Hobbs. "For God's sake will you turn off that drip and get off the line so somebody else can use the phone."

He could hear a gasp at the other end. "Well I never. Did you hear that, May? I've had this phone in fifteen years an' I never seen the beat of that. Call me up after lunch. I'm not going to sit here and be insulted by this—this—" The line went dead.

Eventually he got through to Mrs. Saltonstall. No, Mr. Saltonstall was not in. No, she didn't know when he'd be back. Probably late that night. No, she didn't know just where he was. He was apt to be anywhere in the course of a day the way things went wrong with the summer people. He'd said something about stopping at Davises'. Did Mr. Hobbs know where Davises' was? Well, he couldn't miss it if he took the Oldfleet Road an' watched out for a red panel truck.

An hour later Mr. Hobbs found Davises'. Mr. Saltonstall had been there, but he'd left some time ago. On his way to the Watsons'. Couldn't miss it. Big white house back from the road. Watch for red panel truck.

All the houses in that particular section were white and back from the road. Finally he spied a red panel truck coming out of a driveway about half a mile ahead. It started down the road like a racing car, Mr. Hobbs in hot pursuit.

It was a long chase but at last the red truck drew into a gas station and Mr. Hobbs cornered it.

It was difficult to tell what Mr. Saltonstall looked like, his face being almost hidden by daubs of black grease. He was most friendly. He got out of the panel truck and seized Mr. Hobbs' hand in a greasy clasp. They sat down together on the running board of the truck. Mr. Saltonstall produced cigarette papers and a bag of tobacco from which he fashioned a cigarette with great deliberation. When it was finished it was almost as greasy as the rest of him.

Mr. Hobbs explained his difficulties. Mr. Saltonstall was sympathetic. "My, my," he said. "You *shouldn't* have no trouble. Good pump. Put it in myself. I'll run down bimeby."

"*Couldn't* you come now?" pleaded Mr. Hobbs.

Mr. Saltonstall consulted a greasy gold watch. "I promised Mrs. Cotes I'd be right up to look at her cesspool. Backing up or something. Sure, I'll run over to your place now. Mrs. Cotes can wait."

"You lead the way," said Mr. Hobbs. "I haven't any idea how to get there."

Fifteen minutes later the red panel truck tore into the

driveway of Grey Gables throwing up a shower of gravel. Mr. Hobbs was close behind. Mrs. Hobbs heard the cars and came out on the porch.

"Roger Hobbs, where *have* you been? Don't you know we have to meet Brenda at the two o'clock boat? Really you are very aggravating sometimes. You go off somewhere and get talking—"

Mr. Hobbs interrupted. "Take the car if you think we're going to be late. Meet Brenda yourself," he said. "If I let him out of my sight somebody'll steal him."

Mr. Saltonstall had selected a boxful of tools from the truck and was on his way down to the pumphouse. He looked at the little engine for a long time. "You say she don't start?" he asked finally. He obviously didn't want to attack the problem from the wrong angle due to any misunderstanding.

"It won't start," said Mr. Hobbs.

Mr. Saltonstall spat into the bayberry bushes. Next he spat on his hands and hitched up his blue jeans. He leaned down and poked at the engine with a blackened forefinger while Mr. Hobbs watched anxiously over his shoulder. Then he backed away and pushed the starting lever down with his foot.

The engine coughed once or twice, then settled into a contented purr. "Okay now," said Mr. Saltonstall. "Good engine." He picked up his box of tools. "Got to go now. See Mrs. Cotes. Something the matter with her cesspool. Backing up most likely. Pleased to have metcha."

5

Boat dock

Twice each day the *Island Queen,* a somewhat pregnant-looking car ferry, made the round trip between the Mainland and Long Beach. In its shadowed maw it bore the thousands of oddly assorted articles which the Summer Colony regarded as essential to its existence, while the rails of its upper decks were lined with eager, windswept replacements for the Colony's constantly shifting ranks.

Packed in among the bicycles and the little flat cars piled with cartons and crates, like ships icebound in an arctic sea, were triple rows of shiny convertibles and aristocratic station wagons democratically interspersed among toil-worn jalopies. Each car, whether high born or low, was jammed to the roof with loose personal effects all of which looked curiously alike, an impression which was heightened by the open box of paper handkerchiefs which was standard equipment in every rear window.

A thoughtful observer might have wondered why so many cars were needed on a small island where most of the summer inhabitants were dedicated to a few brief weeks of exercise and health. To the Summer Colony, however, the automobile was just as important as peaked caps, shorts, dark glasses and loud shirts. As a Colony it went in, of course, for outdoor activities of every kind, *but* it liked its exercise to come under the head of Sport. Walking solely for the purpose of getting from one place to another did not fall into this category and was therefore to be avoided like poison ivy.

Long Beach was the port of entry for the Island. It was a kind of a giant sieve in reverse where the smallest units, those who came to the edge of the Mainland on trains and arrived at the Island on their own two feet, became entangled in the town's gingerbread cottages and long boxlike hotels—and went no further. The slim-limbed cyclists adjusted their packs, checked up on their cameras and rode off to the youth hostels which were scattered unobtrusively about the Island. And finally the big convertibles and the station wagons rattled across the loose boards of the dock and whisked away disdainfully in the direction of Rock Harbor and the south shore.

The *Queen,* with a keen sense of her royal status, liked a dash of fanfare with her entrances. One moment she didn't exist to those who stood on the dock, impatiently awaiting her arrival. Nothing appeared as far as the horizon but a few white sails. Then the *Queen* came popping out from behind a wooded point several hundred yards away. At first she proceeded coyly down the shore as if bound for some other place, then with a long, deep-throated hoot of joy, she swung round the last red channel buoy and headed for the dock.

On the upper deck the passengers were crowding toward the bow for a first look at the Island. Old-timers identified familiar landmarks in relieved tones as if they had half expected to find them missing after a winter's absence. "There's Rex's garage. See. The yellow building on the point. You're looking in the wrong place." "There's the Standard Oil tank. Same old Standard Oil tank, by golly." "The old dock hasn't changed, has it?" "No. Same old dock."

The Newcomers mingled with the Old-timers and looked timidly from the speakers to the points indicated on the shore hoping that they also might identify Rex's garage and the Standard Oil tank.

In the faces of the Newcomers might be seen a mixture of childish anticipation and apprehension. To those who were arriving to spend their first summer vacation on the Island the approaching shore represented the realization of a decision reached months ago usually after embattled argument. Now those responsible for these decisions were torn between the high hopes which a strange environment engenders and the knowledge that the product had better be as advertised or it would be the worse for them.

To those who were coming to visit friends "for a few days" the eagerness to experience the new was tempered by the guilty feeling that their pleasure would be considerably enhanced if they could only remain by themselves. To greet their hosts at the pier and then to leave them until the moment for departure arrived—that would be ideal. It was the thought of the days that they must spend with their close and dear friends that caused the worried look in their eyes.

Almost all of the people clustered at the rail shared a common experience. For eleven months they had been looking forward to the week or the fortnight or the month which was now about to begin. For eleven months it had been in the background of their minds—a symbol of the much-vaunted freedom which was the inalienable right of every man, but which became so buried under the responsibilities of life that it was sometimes hard to find.

It was only during this brief period each year that they could hope to truly achieve this freedom—freedom (in theory at least) to do nothing if that was what they chose to do and to do it when and as the spirit moved, unguided by clocks or convention; freedom to do all the things which, during the crowded hours of winter, had seemed so desirable—to dance, to love, to loaf, to listen to a radio on a golden beach, to skim over blue waters in a boat of dazzling white, to read, to walk over fields and moors, to ride sleek horses down wooded trails, to sit on rocks and watch the seas break up in thunder at their feet, to lie on the grass and watch the stately movement of the great white clouds—to just sleep.

These were the dreams, half submerged, which now gave such a look of childish anticipation to the faces lining the rail. To what extent they were to be realized lay in the lap of the next few weeks or days. They did not know, however, that they would never come closer to realization than during those few moments while the *Island Queen* rounded the last channel buoy at reduced speed and headed for its berth.

The scene on the dock was equally colorful. Here were mingled those whose release was over for another year, as well as those in midchannel who were on hand merely for purposes of hail or farewell and, in the background, the usual sprinkling of natives, stolidly engaged in the business of making freedom possible at a reasonable profit.

The departing group was dressed in its store clothes for the first time in many days. The chic hats and the slightly wrinkled suits seemed somehow out of place—the men looked like farmers in their church clothes and many of the women were reminiscent of female impersonators. Perhaps the sun-tanned faces did not blend with city trappings. Perhaps it was the contrast with the multicolored and amazing costumes of those who were remaining. Whatever it was, the congruous had for the moment unaccountably become the incongruous.

They stood about the weather-stained pier in little knots—people who had never seen or heard of one another until a few weeks before and who had grown suddenly to love one another as only those do who are on vacation.

Now that, for some, the time was up, the sadness of separation seemed almost unbearable. Those who remained said they wished that they also might be going in order to be spared the pain of saying "good-by." To think of carrying on alone from this point was intolerable. To those who were leaving the sun had set under a cloud so thick it seemed unlikely that it would ever emerge again.

The last pictures were taken against the background of the dark gray piles. It was so vital to have at least a reproduction of these beloved faces—in spite of the fact that they were so indelibly etched in memory that their outline would never fade.

On returning home the first thing each would do would be to leave the rolls of film with the local druggist to be developed. When the prints were made they would be examined eagerly. "Who's that funny-looking girl standing beside you, George?" "Oh you know. I can't think of her name. She was that red-headed little smarty pants that we never could get rid of."

Then the pictures would be put into an old shoebox with others like them. "Someday" they would be pasted in a book, but usually they remained curled up in their box until their owners moved or some other basic change took place in their lives, when they somehow disappeared.

Among the little groups the last hysterical shrieks were being shrieked over the coy local jokes that seem destined to evolve at the seashore. Those who lived near one another in the winter made eager plans to spend every minute of their time together during the coming months. Those fated to live apart swore to correspond constantly until the happy day when they could come together once more.

Then the dreadful moment arrived (somewhat to everybody's relief) when the *Island Queen,* having disgorged her load, was ready for a refill and the departing ones must pass through the gate. Hysteria rose to crescendo. Those who were departing went aboard and rushed to the upper decks to wave to those on the pier below. At the risk of being impaled on splinters, youths climbed to the tops of piles where, standing like sea gulls, they might be nearer to the loved ones on the upper deck.

People normally tongue-tied—people who under ordinary circumstances were unable to think up one consecutive sentence an hour, were now overcome with a rush of thoughts which must be screamed from dock to pier and back again without being understood by anyone.

The *Island Queen* gave a warning toot as if to say, "All right boys, enough of this." The umbilical cords which had held her to the dock were released with a splash and drawn into the *Queen's* innards—retractable umbilical cords! The propellers began to beat the gray water into salty foam. The sea gulls took up their positions twenty feet behind the stern. A gap showed between the *Queen* and the dock.

"Good-by. Good-by. Don't forget to write. I say DON'T FOR-GET TO WRITE. There's Lizzie. She's standing right behind that man with dark glasses. Good-by, good-by. Don't forget to write. Don't take any wooden money. I say DON'T— Good-by, good-by. That's Joe standing under the smoke stack. What's he waving? What a card! Just between you and me I got a little sick of him toward the end."

The *Queen* was a hundred feet from the dock now—squared away and headed for the Mainland. The Newcomers were already dispersed. The Daily Watchers and the Seers Off straggled slowly back to their various affairs, a few to their hotels and boarding houses to write to the departed dear ones—the first and last of such letters likely to be written. Some went to the movies, some sought their favorite rocking chairs on verandahs and the rest resumed their cease-less promenade up and down Ocean Drive.

The *Island Queen* and its passengers were already for-gotten. Tomorrow the names of many would be hard to remember without reference to an address book.

Mr. and Mrs. Hobbs drove over from Grey Gables to Long Beach to meet Brenda—patient, capable Brenda whose hobby, as Mrs. Hobbs had said so often, was hard work—Brenda whose arrival, Mr. Hobbs declared, would make life civilized once more. By which he meant that Brenda would do the cooking, wash the dishes, clean the house and attend to any other odd jobs that occurred to her active mind.

Brenda was what was known in Mrs. Hobbs' circle of

friends as "a treasure." She had served the Hobbs family in this capacity for so long that she had gradually and quietly taken over until in spite of her grim and unending toil, the Hobbs family had in some mysterious way ended by serving her.

Up to this point Brenda had always taken her vacation at the same time that Mr. and Mrs. Hobbs went away for theirs. This year Mrs. Hobbs had felt that she couldn't run a strange house without help and Brenda had, somewhat unwillingly, been induced to come. Now, as the *Island Queen* creaked and slewed its way into the slip, an uneasy feeling of approaching storm came over her but remained unspoken.

Brenda clutched the rail of the upper deck, her eyes scan-

ning the horizon like one of her Viking ancestors. Streamers of graying hair, whipped about her ears by the fresh breeze, heightened the Valkyrian illusion.

"There she is," cried Mrs. Hobbs, waving her handbag. "Yoo hoo, Brenda." Brenda spotted her, bowed her head with dignity and disappeared from the rail to reappear a few minutes later on the lower deck carrying an enormous yellow suitcase. They met her at the gangplank.

"Did you have a comfortable trip, Brenda?" asked Mrs. Hobbs in the oversolicitous voice she always used with servants, particularly when she felt the ground unsure beneath her feet.

"No ma'am," said Brenda.

They pushed through the crowd to the car and then headed out of town along Ocean Drive. Brenda watched the people milling restlessly up and down its broad sidewalks. She observed the hot popcorn wagons, the saltwater taffy stands, the souvenir shops, the shooting galleries, and the movie theaters. She listened to the harsh stream of jazz that poured from the merry-go-round and the dark recesses of the lobster and steak houses. On the left the calm sea sparkled serenely but Brenda was engrossed by the man-made attractions on her right.

As she gazed at them through the open window the stern lines of her face relaxed. "Nice," she said. "Lotta people. We live here?"

"Well, not right *in* the town, Brenda." Apprehension returned to Mrs. Hobbs' voice. "This is what they call Long Beach. We live a wee wee bit down the road. I don't think you'd like to live right *here*, Brenda."

"Nice," said Brenda, her lips firming.

They left the town behind them and drove through several miles of scrub oak and pine. Brenda looked at it with disapproval. "Like north Sweden," she said. "I guess nobody wants to live this place."

"Oh, these are little *bits* of woods," said Mrs. Hobbs reassuringly. "There are summer people all around here."

Brenda did not contradict her, but continued to stare moodily out the window. At last they came to the moors, rolling treeless to the sea. "Lapp country," said Brenda.

"There's Grey Gables," cried Mrs. Hobbs with the forced enthusiasm which one uses when trying to sell something to a difficult child. "Isn't it lovely, Brenda?" Although the sun had been shining brilliantly when they left Long Beach it was now obliterated by heavy clouds. Grey Gables stood in the midst of a gray world, silhouetted against a slate-gray sea.

"Don't you *love* it, Brenda?" said Mrs. Hobbs hopefully.

"I thank people go crazy in a place like this," said Brenda calmly.

6

It's different than we planned it

As has been mentioned previously, Mr. Hobbs was a dreamer at heart although he would never have admitted it. As an executive it was his responsibility to make stockholders' dreams come true, but such luxuries had no place in his own busy schedule.

From Labor Day on, all through the fall and winter, his feet seldom wandered from the path of duty. No beaver could have led a more dedicated life. With the first touch of spring, however, something within him changed. His imagination, which had given him no trouble for months, suddenly seemed

to escape from its industrial cage and to start soaring back
and forth over the magic month of August.

August! It seemed like such a long and ample period when
considered from the vantage ground of early spring. The
whole of August! In such a space of time it should be possible
to do so many pleasant things.

By the time July came around ideas were crowding in on
him so fast that he began to feel pressed. It was evident that
only by exercising Spartan discipline could he hope to accomplish all that he had in mind. It would be good for him
though—part of the whole, clean picture. He would get up
early—seven o'clock—half past six—why not six? Early bed
and early up. The golden days of August were precious and
not to be wasted.

Now that August had arrived, however, he was aware that
the concept had, somehow or other, gone askew. In the first
place he wasn't getting up as early as planned. He didn't
want to set the alarm clock and disturb Peggy, but without it
he slept like a lump through the beautiful dawn hours to
which he had looked forward. In fact by the time he awoke
Mrs. Hobbs had usually been off about her business for an
hour.

Then, of course, he had not figured on the water pump.
He knew now that he would never master the thing. All he
could hope for was to learn the techniques involved in waging
a running fight with it. There were mornings when he won.
At other times the pump came out ahead. But regardless of
the outcome it was something impossible to reckon with in lay-
ing out a schedule.

After breakfast came the chores. It had never occurred to him that there could be so many routine tasks connected with a house run as simply as Grey Gables.

First he must dump the garbage. Although he did not admit it, this was perhaps his favorite chore for the garbage pit could be a pleasant place on a sparkling, sunny morning.

One walked across the lawn toward the sea to the point where the bayberry bushes took over at the edge of the cliff. A path led through them and over the edge to a little shelf of ground about twenty feet down. Here Mike the Indian, with an eye to beauty as well as utility, had cleared away the bushes and prepared a last resting place for Mr. Hobbs' tin cans and rinds.

It was a spot more suited to a poet's bench than a garbage pit. Grey Gables and all its teeming life were cut off by the bank above. Sixty feet below the waves broke among the streaming boulders. Beyond them the blue sea extended to the sky.

It was a sea gull's view of life. Mr. Hobbs liked to stand beside the pit, looking down on the big, white birds as they circled and glided, with a rhythm so graceful that it was almost music.

A few feet above the pit the remains of an old stone wall broke through the thicket of bushes. There a community of crows made their headquarters. Whenever they saw Mr. Hobbs coming across the lawn with his pail they took up their positions on the mossy stones and watched his movements with beady eyes.

Mr. Hobbs would empty the pail into the pit and then

spread a neat, thin layer of red earth over everything. His work done he would lean on the long handle of the rusty shovel absorbing the scene and feeling its tranquillity seep through his pores.

The crows, who were used to all this beauty and lived with its tranquillity for twelve months of the year, regarded such daydreaming with impatience. It was what might be expected of animals who threw good food into a hole and covered it up with dirt. They sat motionless and unblinking until Mr. Hobbs had climbed up the path. Then, leaving one of their group to stand guard on the wall, they swooped into the pit from which they emerged a few minutes later grasping their plunder in claw and beak.

Weighted down with grapefruit rinds and pieces of burnt toast they rose heavily into the air like overloaded bombers and dispersed over the countryside. Eventually most of them became either exhausted or bored and dropped their burdens on the roofs and lawns of the summer folk, after which they returned to the stone wall to sleep and think the matter over.

After Mr. Hobbs had lined the garbage pail with fresh newspapers—a task in which he came to take an artist's creative pride—his next duty was to collect the contents of all scrap baskets and burn them in an old oil drum which stood just behind the pumphouse.

This was also a pleasant spot, cut off from the world above and overlooking the sea and the little cove. In addition to enjoying the view, Mr. Hobbs had a secret passion for burning things. It fascinated him to drop lighted matches into the rusty drum and watch the tiny points of flame fighting for existence, finding a corner of paper to feed upon, growing suddenly in strength, pushing up underneath cartons, through the chinks of which thick yellow smoke poured into the clear air. He watched the tops of the cartons turn slowly brown until finally the flames burst through and their sides settled, writhing and formless, into the inferno.

It was like visitors' day at the Spanish Inquisition. There was usually a paper napkin which lay miraculously unscathed in the midst of the fire. Mr. Hobbs felt rather sorry when it finally exploded into flame and was gone. Then he looked at his wrist watch and hurried up the hill like a small boy who has been caught doing something particularly foolish.

Then there were the bottles. Mr. Hobbs had never realized how many empty bottles an American family produces each day. Their disposal had presented a problem until he discovered a clump of sumac bushes halfway down the path to the cove from the center of which emerged a steeple-shaped rock. It was a wonderful target for empty bottles and whether he hit it or not didn't really matter as everything disappeared eventually into the sumac. He occasionally varied his routine by throwing an empty into the air and trying to hit it with a second one before both disappeared into the matted undergrowth. He had to be careful, of course, that someone coming down the path to the cove did not interrupt one of these exhibitions, but this slight element of danger only made the game more interesting.

These were his routine duties. They were neither arduous nor complex, but it was amazing how much time he could spend on them. After some experience a good planner of days should have been able to take such things into account and adjust his schedule accordingly. It was the casual odds and ends, however, the unforeseeable flotsam and jetsam of daily living that really derailed his plans.

"I've got to go down to the village, dear. It would help a lot if you'd come with me. I have to drop the laundry at Mrs. Maroni's and I can't struggle with that basket."

"Where in the world is Kate?" asked Mr. Hobbs crossly. "Doesn't that child have any part in this performance at all?"

"Roger, I don't think you'd notice if your family disappeared into thin air. Kate spent the night with the Sandhursts after the dance. And anyway, this is the child's vacation."

Mr. Hobbs looked at her, but said nothing.

These trips to Rock Harbor were a constant source of bewilderment and financial anguish to him. "Why in the world you can't clean this whole mess up once a week, Peggy, and then forget it for the other six days is more than I can understand."

It sounded easy, but each day seemed to bring some sort of a crisis which inevitably involved a trip to the village. And regardless of what trifling item had made the journey necessary the car always returned to Grey Gables with the usual number of big cartons lined up on the back seat, each bulging with miscellaneous household musts of which toilet paper always seemed to have been the last article packed. They never varied in size or weight and Mr. Hobbs eventually became convinced that if Mrs. Hobbs ran a continuous shuttle service to Rock Harbor this would still be true.

As he staggered between the car and the kitchen with these

ungainly burdens he never ceased to wonder where all this merchandise was going. It was like pouring water into a sieve, only more expensive. Each day he carried great piles of food and equipment to the kitchen table. Each day he delivered a small pail of garbage to the crows, burned a few papers and hurled a few empties into the bushes.

A large ruled pad lay on the living-room table. On this Mrs. Hobbs kept a running list of needed things. Hour by hour during the day it grew in length. "Put down catsup, will you dear, while you're sitting there."

"I'm not 'sitting there.' I'm reading," said Mr. Hobbs, "and what's more I saw about three bottles of catsup coming in yesterday. Good lord, Peggy, what do you do with the stuff—flush the drains with it?"

"Darling, it doesn't make any difference *when* we bought catsup. The point is it's all gone *now*. And we don't pour it down the drain. Just write down two bottles of catsup and stop fussing about things that are not in your department."

Mr. Hobbs muttered something about his department having to go on three shifts to pay for the wastage of other departments—and made the notation.

Mrs. Hobbs was standing by the kitchen sink. "Roger, while you're doing nothing will you put down a pencil sharpener and a bread knife. Oh yes, and a paper towel holder."

"Good God, isn't this house equipped with anything? What do you mean a paper towel holder?"

"One of these metal things to hold rolls of paper towels. Like this."

"What's the matter with that one?"

"Every time you try to tear off a paper towel the roll falls into the sink. Look." Mrs. Hobbs pulled at a paper towel and, as predicted, the roll disengaged itself and fell into the dishpan with a splash. "See."

Mr. Hobbs made the requested memoranda. "If you knew it was going to fall in the water that was a silly thing to do," he said.

Having failed to reduce the number of these expeditions to the village Mr. Hobbs tried to introduce some efficiency into them, hoping in this way to salvage a few of the hours when he should have been lying on sun-baked sands or walking over lonely moors.

On the way into town he made a second list of all the items which Mrs. Hobbs considered him mentally capable of buying. Then he rushed through his purchases, beginning at one end of the business section and ending at the other exhausted, but with a sense of accomplishment.

Having piled his packages in the back of the car he would go in search of Mrs. Hobbs, whom he usually found either at the A & P or Frisbee's Market standing before a great heap of merchandise which perspiring young men in soiled white aprons were enlarging every minute.

"Almost through, dear?"

"Gracious no. I've got a million more things. Why don't you go and sit in the car and read? You'll make me nervous if you stand there fidgeting."

"But do you know what time it is?"

"I can't *help* it, Roger. If you want to eat someone has to buy the food. Oh yes—that reminds me—I'm going to need more money. Why don't you give me your wallet and then all I have to do is tell you how much I've spent."

It was disconcerting but Mr. Hobbs hoped that when Mrs. Hobbs finally got the place stocked up and running his days would become more orderly. Then he might find time for some of his more important projects.

For the moment, however, things were not working out quite as he had planned.

Mr. Hobbs looked forward to the arrival of his two married daughters and their families. Then everything would fall into the groove. As he thought of the happy hours that he would spend with his grandchildren a warm glow of anticipation permeated his being.

7

The social season starts

Mr. and Mrs. Hobbs drove silently back from Long Beach. They had just put Brenda on the boat for the Mainland. After gazing over the limitless blue ocean for a week she had expressed her judgment on Grey Gables and the verdict was unfavorable.

Brenda had been brought up in North Sweden which, she admitted, was a lonely and sparsely settled country. Compared with Grey Gables, however, it had been positively congested. At least, as Brenda said, "There vas a *few* peoples and vunce in a vile you heard a vulf."

She was returning to Cleveland to visit a brother who lived in an overcrowded house in an overcrowded part of the city. There she would relax until the Hobbs family reappeared after Labor Day.

"It won't be so bad," said Mrs. Hobbs with forced cheeriness, "when Susan and Jane get here with the children. Then everybody can pitch in. In the meanwhile Kate's out most of the time and it will be kind of fun to picnic by ourselves."

An immense depression settled over Mr. Hobbs.

Later that day he went upstairs to wash his hands.

He had been collecting some large rocks down at the cove. These he had placed in a neat row around the edges of the driveway in a final attempt to keep the milkman off the crab grass. Later he would whitewash them, but staggering up the steep path under their dead weight had been heavy work. He felt tired and drowsy. After he had cleaned up a bit it might be pleasant to stretch out on his bed for a few minutes.

He placed the rubber stopper in the bowl, washed his hands with sleepy care and removed the stopper. To his surprise the water did not revolve clockwise down the drain in the mysterious manner of well-regulated water. Instead a column of brown liquid shot up from the bottom of the bowl to the level of Mr. Hobbs' astonished nose.

He jumped back in alarm, never having seen anything quite like this outside of Yellowstone Park. The geyser subsided and from the drainpipe came a series of throaty noises from somewhere far below. They were the sort of noises that might have been made by a dying sea serpent.

"But Roger, I don't see how water could *jump* at you out of a drainpipe. It does seem to me this house acts very peculiarly—and with Brenda gone and everything. Have you called Mr. Cabot, or whatever the plumber's name is?"

Mrs. Saltonstall did not know where her husband was. He

had been out on jobs since early morning. Yes, if he called in she would tell him. It sounded to her like maybe a cesspool backing up.

This was the first time that Mr. Hobbs had given any thought to what happened to the immense quantities of water which flowed from his home each day. His concern to date had been to get the water *into* it. In the primitive world in which he now lived, however, water appeared to be a two-way problem.

Judging from what he knew about Fred Saltonstall the man might not show up for days. In the meantime no one knew what hellish things might be concocting in the bowels of the earth beneath him. He decided to do some preliminary research, although he realized that this was not without danger to himself in case of a major eruption.

Grey Gables had no cellar. It sat close to the ground on a foundation of concrete blocks. Mr. Hobbs had noticed a small wooden panel set into the foundation wall near the kitchen door. He approached this now with unwilling feet, removed the boards and, lying on his stomach, waved a flashlight back and forth into the darkness. The narrow beam of the light picked up a broken express wagon, some firewood, numerous wooden piles on which the house appeared to be resting and an occasional section of iron pipe. Mr. Hobbs wriggled through the hole like a stout snake and disappeared into a strange, uncharted world.

At just about the time that he had gone upstairs to wash his hands Mrs. Archer Gabrielson had stepped daintily across the ancient millstone that formed the doorstep of her historic colonial house which, for almost two hundred years, had looked out over the peaceful waters of Rock Harbor.

Her smartly slippered feet crunched along the flower-bordered path, passed through the gate of a snow-white picket fence, entered a dark green convertible and took their places on the foot pedals.

Everything about Mrs. Archer Gabrielson was smart; her clothes, her hair, her car and the very way she drove it. As she guided it nonchalantly down the narrow one-way village street, miraculously missing children on bicycles and long lines of parked fenders, her smartness was acknowledged by a kind of running ovation from her fellow townsmen. To the greetings of the Summer Colony she waved and smiled in one way. To the more restrained greetings of the tradesmen she waved and smiled in a slightly different way.

A stranger, watching her progress, would have concluded that Mrs. Archer Gabrielson not only knew everybody in Rock Harbor, but also that in some subtle manner she was the pivot around which that compact little community re-volved. He would have been correct.

At the end of the street she brought the car to a halt beside Mr. Kenneth Wainwright, disregarding the fact that by so doing she had immobilized traffic for four blocks behind her. Mr. Kenneth Wainwright was Mrs. Gabrielson's fill-in man and one of the few summer residents of Rock Harbor who, at the age of fifty-five, could cross his knees like Clifton Webb. As he leaned on the door of the convertible it was clear that he had been born to scenes like this. Everything about him fell naturally into place, from his white cable-stitch sweater, to his immaculate white shorts and snug-fitting Bermuda stockings.

"Yes, it's really quite ghastly," Mrs. Gabrielson was saying, "but Retta took all the trouble to write me about these people so I suppose it's up to me to do something about it."

"Would you like a bodyguard?" asked Mr. Wainwright.

Mrs. Gabrielson laughed, a light, tinkling laugh which harmonized perfectly with her costume and the convertible. "No," she said. "I must face my ordeal alone. I went to school with this Mrs. Whatshername although I can't remember what she looked like." The blowing of horns behind her had grown threatening. "I seem to be holding somebody up," she said. "See you at the Marstons'."

She moved forward and the traffic of Main Street resumed its flow. Once clear of the village she turned west along the shore road in the direction of Grey Gables, looking a bit bored as she always did when following the path of duty and uncertain just where it was leading.

As she had told Kenneth Wainwright, Peggy Richards had gone to Sweethorn Hall with her. Peggy had been a year ahead of her. They had never met since, and many things could have happened in the intervening years and probably had. She vaguely remembered that Peggy had married some butter-and-egg man from Cleveland. That was all she knew. At any rate, here they were, and it was up to her to do something about it because she was Mrs. Archer Gabrielson. Peggy Richards had suddenly become an occupational hazard.

Mrs. Hobbs poked her head into the opening through which her husband had disappeared. She was on her hands

and knees, her sleeves were rolled up, wisps of hair hung across her eyes and there was consternation in her voice.

"Roger. For pity's sake stop fooling around in that place and attend to things. There's a convertible coming up the drive with the top down." In the kitchen above, a buzzer sounded.

The voice from underneath the house was muffled. "Listen, Peggy, what am I supposed to be—butler and plumber and everything else in this place. What's the matter? Have you got convertible phobia or what?"

"Oh dear, this is dreadful." The shadow of Mrs. Hobbs' body disappeared from the opening. Mr. Hobbs wriggled into a new position and continued his inspection.

"I never was more glad to see anyone, Polly, but I couldn't be more embarrassed to have you catch me like this. You see our maid left this morning.—We only had one," she added lamely.

"You poor dear," said Mrs. Archer Gabrielson, taking in every detail of Mrs. Hobbs' appearance. "I couldn't be sorrier for you. What a heavenly view."

Mrs. Archer Gabrielson seated herself daintily in one of the wicker porch chairs. Mrs. Hobbs felt like a child who has been delegated to make a guest comfortable in her parents' absence.

"It's been so long," Mrs. Archer Gabrielson was saying, "so unbelievably long since those lovely days at Sweethorn. We were *so* silly, weren't we. I used to be scared to death of you because you were one of the old girls."

Mrs. Hobbs bridled slightly. "I was only a year ahead of you," she said.

"Oh my dear, it must have been more than that. You were *ages* ahead of me. I was *terrified* of you and then you were married, weren't you, and went to live out west somewhere—"

"Cleveland," said Mrs. Hobbs.

"Cleveland," agreed Mrs. Gabrielson. "And we lost all touch with one another and now it's going to be such fun to have you here, only I wish you were not so far away from things, and I'm dying to meet your nice husband."

Mrs. Hobbs started. From where she was seated she could see the west window of the living room. A curtain had been lifted cautiously and in the narrow opening a face had appeared—or rather a mask of red earth pierced by two glaring eyes. As the eyes met hers the face vanished and the curtain fell back into place.

"I must go and find him," said Mrs. Hobbs. "He's puttering around somewhere. And you *will* have a cup of tea, won't you?"

Mrs. Archer Gabrielson lifted a white-gloved hand. "Not a thing, my dear. But I *do* want to meet that man of yours. It seems so funny to think of you married. I won't believe it till I see him."

"You have a boat of course," said Mrs. Gabrielson.

There was a streak of dirt still visible in Mr. Hobbs' hair and a large brown patch of the stuff behind his ear which looked like a birthmark. By and large, however, he had done a creditable job under pressure. Now, with his fingers curved around a Scotch and soda, he began to feel more relaxed even to the point of being aware of Mrs. Archer Gabrielson's sophisticated charm. To Mrs. Hobbs' surprise he said he'd been thinking about a boat. He just hadn't done anything about it, however.

"But, my dear, it's a 'must' in Rock Harbor. *Everybody* has a boat. That nice daughter of yours that I want so much to meet is going to use it every day. Do you sail a great deal?"

Mr. Hobbs replied modestly that he'd done quite a bit of crewing in his day.

"Roger has been in the Bermuda race," said Mrs. Hobbs.

"Oh, then you're a real deepwater sailor," said Mrs. Gabrielson. "These little class boats of ours will probably bore the life out of you. They're just racing toys. Why don't you get a little boat for the children to race in and then charter something bigger for yourself?"

Mr. Hobbs said there was so much to do in Rock Harbor that he didn't think he'd have time for more than one boat.

"Then I have just the thing for you," said Mrs. Gabrielson. "You'll want a Spatterbox."

"A what?" asked Mr. Hobbs.

"A Spatterbox. That's what they call our little racing class here. They're very simple. We try to keep everything very simple. But they're nice little boats. There must be twenty of them. They race every Wednesday and Saturday. You'll have lots of fun racing with your children if they'll let you. Mine won't, thank God. Reg McHugh's got a Spatterbox and there's nobody at his house to sail it during August so he wants to charter it. I'm seeing him at a cocktail party this afternoon and I'll manage everything."

"I'd certainly like to look it over," said Mr. Hobbs cautiously.

"Nothing to look at," said Mrs. Gabrielson. "They're all alike. Just take it. You're lucky to get one. I'll take it for you when I see Reg. It's so beautiful here. So primitively wild."

From below the edge of the cliff three crows rose heavily, silhouetted against the blue background of the sea. Their talons were fastened on gleaming objects which Mr. Hobbs knew had just been excavated from his garbage pit. He wished that one of them would jettison its freight in Mrs. Gabrielson's immaculate convertible.

"How much—" he began.

"Oh gracious, I don't know how much," said Mrs. Gabrielson. Her voice indicated that such matters were not discussed by certain people. "You can arrange all that with Reg. Then of course you'll want to join our little Yacht Club. It's very simple and quite charming. That won't be any trouble because Reg is Commodore and naturally if you charter his boat he'll be glad to put you up. And then you'll want to rent—"

Mr. Hobbs never learned what the third thing was, for at that moment a red panel truck skidded into the driveway and made a polo pony stop before the house. Mr. Saltonstall got out and came over to the porch.

"Well well," he said. "My missus tells me the cesspool's blowed up in your face. Howdo, Mrs. Gabrielson. That water closet of yours stopped dripping yet? I tied a piece of copper wire round the ball cock. I guess it oughta hold till the new part comes. If it don't you can take the tank cover off and take up on it with a pair of pliers. So you think they's something th' matter with th' cesspool, eh? Shouldn't be. Built it myself. Well, I'll stroll around an' have a look at it. You might want to come with me, Mr. Hobbs."

"If you'll excuse me I think I will," said Mr. Hobbs.

"Might be as the dang thing's filled up," said Mr. Salton-stall. "You get a lot of people in a house like this an' it don't take long."

When Mr. Hobbs returned the convertible had gone.

"We're going to Polly's for cocktails tomorrow," said Mrs. Hobbs. "She's giving a party."

"You can count me out," said Mr. Hobbs with decision. But he knew he would be there.

8

Over the bounding main

It might be said that Mr. Hobbs and family were now officially accepted as members of Rock Harbor's Summer Colony.

A cocktail party, which Mrs. Archer Gabrielson had been planning to give in any event, had been designated by her as the vehicle for introducing them to their fellow Colonists.

Mr. Hobbs told Mrs. Hobbs that under no circumstances would he let himself in for any such rat race. He had come to the Island for rest and relaxation and didn't propose to get tangled up in this kind of twa-ti-twa.

Having asserted his individuality, he tried on three possible costumes, chose one which later proved to be 100 per cent

64

wrong, found on arrival that he didn't know anybody just as he had foretold, tried to make up for this deficiency by drinking a number of martinis in quick succession and eventually agreed to rent a boat from a man whose name was either McHugh or McAdoo and to join the Rock Harbor Yacht Club. When he arrived home he realized that he hadn't asked the cost of either and went to bed shortly afterward.

As Mrs. Hobbs said, however, if one came to a place like Rock Harbor one really should be a part of it.

The Yacht Club was a disappointment to him, although he had no preconceived ideas about such places. It occupied a weather-beaten building which had, apparently, once been a sail loft and which contained a single, bare room. A battered upright piano and the garish shields of a jazz orchestra standing on a low platform in one corner, plus a few folding chairs, were its only furnishings.

"What a charming room," said Mrs. Hobbs.

A pier ran from the clubhouse out into the harbor, terminating in a float. The pier served as a hitching rail for a long row of assorted dinghies. A few yards out in the harbor, bobbing violently at their moorings, were the sailboats, including Mr. Hobbs' Spatterbox which carried the name *Dashaway* on its stern.

With Mrs. Hobbs and Kate he leaned on the rail at the end of the pier and surveyed his property gloomily. Unfortunately at that miserable cocktail party Mr. McHugh (or McAdoo) had asked him if he was a sailor man. He had indicated, with becoming modesty, that he knew a bit about such matters, which had eventually led him to give McHugh-McAdoo and a group of others a blow-by-blow account of his Bermuda race.

It had been a fatal mistake. When they were leaving Mr. Hobbs had suggested that McHugh-McAdoo take him for a trial run the next morning in *Dashaway* for the purpose of showing him the ropes. Like so many sailor men, however, McHugh-McAdoo was one of those objectionably rough-and-ready types who are always simplifying life—for themselves at least.

"Nonsense," he had roared. "You're an old Bermuda man. You don't need me. *Dashaway*'s a child's boat—a toy. Just take her out and get the feel of her. You've been used to big stuff. You're going to get quite a kick out of something that re-sponds like *Dashaway*. Good little boat. You may find she has too much weather helm, but you'll get used to that in no time."

Mr. Hobbs had said he was sure he would and the strange thing was that at the moment, and without having the dimmest

idea what weather helm meant, he had believed it. Now, as he watched *Dashaway's* mast swinging crazily among a grove of other thrashing spars, he began to have doubts of his sanity.

Kate was tugging at his coat. "Come on, Pops. Don't let's stand here all day. Let's go."

"Yes, Rog. Let's go for a ride in it. We've got to learn about it sometime."

"First of all you don't 'go for a ride' in a boat," said Mr. Hobbs. "You go for a sail. And secondly you don't take a little racing shell like that out in a gale like this."

They looked disappointed. At that moment two little girls with pigtails accompanied by a fat boy came noisily down the pier. While the Hobbses watched they threw a sailbag into one of the dinghies, dropped into it casually from the runway of the pier, cast off and rowed out to one of the boats. In a few

minutes their sail was flapping and slatting. The fat boy let go the mooring and the little craft, heeling far over, slipped through the fleet into the open harbor, followed by a hopeful gull.

"Well," said Mr. Hobbs uneasily. "I guess we'd better be going back."

"Listen, Pops. Those little girls couldn't have been more than twelve years old. If they can go out, we can."

"Come on, dear. Let's go out. We can help you."

"You're not scared are you, Pops?"

They went back to the clubhouse and got their bag of sails and a pair of oars. Mr. Hobbs tried to whistle cheerily as he threw the sailbag over his shoulder. He felt that was what the picture called for. Internally, however, he felt physically sick as they lowered themselves into the dinghy.

The trip out to *Dashaway* was a nightmare. The dinghy had apparently been built for small children. Three full-size people weighed it down almost to the waterline. What had looked like sparkling wavelets from the pier suddenly became a menacing sea which slapped viciously against the sides of the tiny craft and hurled water over Mrs. Hobbs' ankles.

"Rog, couldn't you row so that all the waves don't come inside? I don't want to ruin these shoes."

"What in the world do you want to wear shoes like that for on a boat?" grunted Mr. Hobbs.

He glanced over his shoulder. The *Dashaway* was only a few feet from them, tugging at its mooring line like a trapped animal and rocking back and forth so violently that her mast seemed to slap the water on either side.

Mr. Hobbs looked despairingly at Mrs. Hobbs sitting calmly in the rear of the dinghy with her hands over her shoes. Wouldn't someone put a stop to this suicidal expedition?

"This is fun," said Mrs. Hobbs. She removed her shoes and tossed them gaily into *Dashaway's* cockpit.

Mr. Hobbs could never remember how they managed to transfer from the tossing dinghy to the tossing sailboat. It was one of those feats of the sea which he had read about as a boy but never expected to participate in—one of those incredible acts of derring-do that he associated with the movies and adventure novels rather than industrialists from Cleveland.

He straddled the centerboard box and shook the sails out of the bag. "Now," he said, in what he hoped was a casual tone, "if someone will hand me the main halyard."

"The what?"

"The rope that you tie onto the top of the sail to hoist it up."

"Why didn't you say so, dear? Where on earth do they keep it?"

A ganglia of ropes were slapping angrily against the mast. Shielding his eyes Mr. Hobbs looked up at the masthead which was behaving like an inverted pendulum. He was immediately forced to clutch the edge of the tiny half deck until the dizziness left him.

By tugging gently on each rope he eventually discovered one with a free end which had been hooked to the turnbuckle of a shroud. He unhooked it and inched his way cautiously back to the cockpit. It was a job requiring both hands. As a result the halyard slipped away from him and flew out into space only to come flailing back past his head with the next roll of the boat.

"Gracious," said Mrs. Hobbs, "shouldn't that thing be tied to something?"

"Catch hold of it," said Mr. Hobbs, "and hold it till I'm ready for it." He immediately devoted his attention to the pile of canvas at his feet. The jib was easy to identify. He handed it to Kate. "You put that on," he said.

"How?"

"Darling, you've got to work it out. Now don't be helpless. Just go and work it out."

He passed the edges of the mainsail through his fingers until he came to a corner. That might be the top. He continued along the edge. Another corner. *That* could be the top. Good Lord, here was another corner. Why didn't they mark the darn thing "Back," "Front" and "Top." Maybe it didn't make any difference which you used.

A dinghy passed containing two little girls who waved at *Dashaway.* "Nice breeze," they called. Mr. Hobbs watched them with astonishment as they leaped casually aboard the next boat and went about the business of putting on the sail.

Ah that was it! The top was the corner with the black number sewn just below it. Of course. How stupid. And the part that went along the mast had those little zipper things. Now he was getting the hang of it. He worked in frantic haste, lest his models sail away and leave him helpless once more.

Somehow or other the sails were on and up, slatting savagely as if resenting such amateur handling.

One of the little girls in the next boat took the tiller, the other went forward and cast off the mooring line. Their boat turned its cheek to the breeze with lazy grace, its sails filled and it went dancing across *Dashaway's* bow. "Race?" called the little girl at the tiller.

"You bet," shouted Mr. Hobbs. "Meet you out there." He tried to make his voice sound hearty and jovial, but it came out high-pitched and strained. Calm, Hobbs. In emergencies the leader must be calm.

"Now," he said, "untie the dinghy from the stern and tie it to the mooring can. Give it plenty of rope." He felt immensely pleased with himself as Kate carried out this order.

"You're wonderful," said Mrs. Hobbs admiringly.

"Cast off," he said nonchalantly. It was the nonchalance of an actor saying "So long" to his pals in the big battle scene as he steps from his cozy dugout into a rain of shell fire.

Kate's voice came back to him on the wind. "I can't untie this slimy rope from the tin can."

"Don't untie it for God's sake," he shouted. "Throw the tin can over with the rope."

"Don't you want it again?" asked Mrs. Hobbs. She had taken her place on the floor of the cockpit, one arm clinging to the centerboard box.

There was no time to be sarcastic. He heard the splash of the can buoy. Instead of veering off gracefully to the left as the other boat had done, *Dashaway's* sails continued to slat as it drifted down wind, threatening to swamp the dinghy.

"Why do you back out?" asked Mrs. Hobbs.

Mr. Hobbs did not bother to answer. He was pumping the tiller savagely. *Dashaway* suddenly lay down on its beam end and darted for the point where the little fleet was thickest.

"We're skidding," said Mrs. Hobbs.

It was true. *Dashaway* was going sideways through the water almost as fast as it went forward. This two-dimensional progress frustrated Mr. Hobbs more than anything that had happened to date.

"Pops, you're going to hit that boat off to the left if you don't stop drifting."

Drifting! It came to him suddenly. "The centerboard," he screamed. "Will *somebody* drop the centerboard. I can't do everything."

"What are you yelling about?" said Mrs. Hobbs. "Don't yell at me, please. Just tell me quietly what to do."

"The center—" began Mr. Hobbs. "Listen, Peggy. Undo that rope just under your right hand. That's it. It's just twisted around that gadget. That's it. Then let the board down slow—"

Mrs. Hobbs screamed as the rope tore through her hands and then let it go. The knot at the end hit the slot in the centerboard with a thud that shook the boat. The rope held.

"Is that what you wanted?" asked Mrs. Hobbs. "It felt to me as if the bottom fell out. The thing almost took my hand off."

Mr. Hobbs' clenched teeth caused the muscles in his jaw to protrude. *Dashaway* had stopped going sideways, but it was now tearing through the water like a torpedo, pointed at four of its bobbing sister boats. In one of them two young men stopped putting on their sails to watch.

"Why don't you go around those boats?" asked Mrs. Hobbs. "There's no hurry. We've got all day. Gracious sake, Rog, we almost hit them."

Beneath the sail Mr. Hobbs caught a glimpse of the pale, gaping faces of the two youths as *Dashaway* flashed past their stern. Then they were miraculously through the fleet with nothing ahead but the dancing waters of the bay.

Kate came back to get out of the spray. "Gosh, Pops, I didn't know you could sail like that. I wouldn't have had the nerve to go through that mess of boats."

"Your father sailed in a Bermuda race, dear," said Mrs. Hobbs. "I have perfect confidence in him."

Mr. Hobbs did not hear. His mind was elsewhere. *Dash-away* was booming along with the wind almost behind it. Astern the white houses of Rock Harbor were already becoming fused by distance. Half a mile ahead and to the right was a rocky point. He decided that they would clear it nicely. Far ahead to the left was the lighthouse on the end of the sand spit which marked the harbor entrance.

They were headed straight for the open sea. Nothing to worry about, nothing to do but hold her as she was and relax. He threw back his head and enjoyed the movement of the wind in his hair, the same wind that had played in the hair of Drake and Frobisher, Magellan and Cook and all the rest of that carefree band which had once roamed these waters—or at least waters which were very similar.

Kate lay stretched out on the forward deck, engrossed in

her ceaseless struggle to be more sunburned than any other girl in America. Mrs. Hobbs sat on the floor of the cockpit, her face glowing with excitement and pleasure.

"Oh Rog, I don't see why we don't do this all the time," she said dreamily.

A half hour passed. Suddenly Mr. Hobbs' grip on the tiller tightened. The unpleasant thought had just occurred to him that sooner or later he must go back. At the moment he was issuing from the neck of a funnel into unlimited space. Ultimately he must return to the funnel, against the wind, his goal no longer the open ocean but a tiny white can buoy bobbing in the center of a score of boats.

At the thought of dashing into that melee and picking up his mooring in this howling gale, panic seized him. Rather than endure that humiliation under the critical eyes of a lot of little fat girls in pigtails he would turn when the time came, head straight for shore and make a crash landing on the rocks. Or would it be better to keep on going, straight out to sea and eventually get picked up by a passing freighter?

Steady. You're in a tight place. Think it through, boy. What would Magellan and Drake have done now?

At least it would be prudent to practice coming about while he had plenty of room for error. Slowly he brought *Dashaway* up into the wind until she was heading for the long sand spit that formed the south side of the harbor.

"Hard a lee," he said.

"What did you say?" asked Mrs. Hobbs.

"We're coming about."

"What do I do?"

"Nothing."

She settled back contentedly into her corner. Kate raised a protesting face from the deck canvas. "Oh Pops, just when I was getting comfortable!"

"When we come around come back and let go the left-hand jib sheet and take in the right-hand jib sheet," said Mr. Hobbs sternly.

"Your father always likes to make things so complicated," said Mrs. Hobbs. The boat swung to port and she slid away from the centerboard box and fetched up against the side of the cockpit. "Rog, for goodness' sake what are you doing! I was just getting used to that corner and now look what you've done. No one could sit here and you don't get any sun or anything. Can't you tip it back the way it was?"

Mr. Hobbs sailed on, unheeding. His mind had become a great navigating chart on which he was plotting the steps necessary to bring his loved ones safely back to that can buoy. If he ever made it he swore silently that he would never detach *Dashaway* from it again. He gave Kate the tiller and went forward to work on the problem with matches laid out on the canvas deck.

Finally, feeling as Einstein must have when he produced the equation which should unlock the universe, he took back the tiller. He headed for Rock Harbor, the wind on his starboard beam. A few hundred yards away the mast tops of the Spatterbox fleet continued to trace crazy arcs against the sky.

Now the first boats of the fleet were just to leeward. He hadn't realized how fast they were tearing through the water until the little white hulls gave him something against which to measure his speed.

He forced himself to rehearse once more the plan which he

had worked out so carefully. He was to run past the fleet as he was now until he came abreast of his mooring can. Then he was to let the sail out as far as it would go and at the same time make a right angle turn to the left and head a little to the right of the mooring can. Then, just after he had passed the can, he must swing *Dashaway* smartly into the wind and let it come up to the mooring on its momentum. Next he must drop the mainsail while Kate hooked the can with the boat hook. It was really a beautiful maneuver. He wondered at himself for having worked it out.

Now they were among the boats. The boom scraped the shrouds of one. They missed another by inches. Then they were abreast of the mooring.

"Ready with the boat hook, Kate."

"I don't see how you do it," said Mrs. Hobbs.

His chest swelled with pride at the compliment as he shot *Dashaway* into the wind with a flourish and coasted past the dinghy on the leeward side. Kate lay in the bow straining toward the can with the boat hook.

Dashaway went slower and slower and came to a stop a few feet away from the mooring. Then like a playful terrier it turned to the right and went flying across the rope connecting the dinghy to the can. He felt the rope go under the boat and apparently catch on the centerboard. They came to a straining halt with the dinghy glued to their right side and the mooring can to their left.

"What a funny thing," said Mrs. Hobbs.

"Let down the mainsail," roared Mr. Hobbs. No one paid the slightest attention. He leaped for the halyard and loosed

it from the cleat, but the force of the breeze held the sail rigidly in place.

Then he had another inspiration. If he pulled up the centerboard the rope would slide along the bottom of the boat and they would be free. Shoving Mrs. Hobbs' cringing body to one side he pulled it up. *Dashaway* lurched forward a few feet then stuck again.

"What *do* you suppose?" said Mrs. Hobbs.

Kate had come aft and was peering over the stern. "The rope's caught between the stern and the rudder," she said. "I can see it."

"Never again," cried Mr. Hobbs dramatically. "Never again will I come out with a gang that know nothing whatsoever about sailing. The best man in the world couldn't handle a boat in a blow like this without *some* help. This ends it, I tell you. I'm getting rid of the boat—"

Kate had taken off her shoes and stockings. Pushing her father gently aside she lowered herself over the stern. Straddling the rudder she began to work the rope down with her feet. In a few moments they were free.

Dashaway immediately came up into the wind like a colt which gets tired of eluding its pursuers. Mr. Hobbs had forgotten to make the halyard fast, as a result of which the sail fell over their heads in voluminous folds. They were drifting down wind on one of the boats. It was occupied by the two little girls who had wanted to race. They stopped putting the cover on their sail and watched the approach of *Dashaway* with open mouths.

Mr. Hobbs had tasted the dregs of the cup.

9

Anticipation

It was too bad in a way, as Mrs. Hobbs said, that the Carvers and the Grants were arriving at the same time, but she supposed young people had to take their vacations when they could and probably it would be more fun for the men to be here together. When they left she and Mr. Hobbs would have Susan and Jane and the grandchildren all to themselves for the rest of the month. Then, she said without explaining why, things wouldn't be nearly so confusing.

Mr. Hobbs agreed. He was in an agreeing mood, for in a short while his rapidly expanding family would be gathered together for the first time in over a year. He had always looked forward to the grandfather period of his life, to reliving his early married days through a second generation, to watching its growth and development from day to day and, perhaps, to having some small part in shaping it.

Now, for a few weeks at least, all these things would be possible.

In his moments of anticipation there was always an image in his mind of himself and Susan's four-year-old Peter, rambling over the countryside hand in hand. It was probably inspired by a book of A. A. Milne which he used to read to the girls when they were little. In it there was a drawing of a man and a small boy walking on a beach. The boy had curly hair framing an angel's face. He was holding the man's hand and, as Mr. Hobbs remembered the text, they were engaged in one of those extraordinary and charming conversations which seem to come so naturally either to English children or to the Englishmen who write about them.

Whether or not he had been influenced by this picture, Mr. Hobbs had gradually created an idyll in which he and Peter were the two principal characters—the man and the boy walking together—exploring, observing, learning, the one from the other. It was a vision of peace and order—a fusing of the two extremes of life into something rich and full.

All of which should not be taken to mean that Mr. Hobbs did not love his other two grandchildren deeply and tenderly. He did, of course, but little Peewee was only a year old when Mr. Hobbs had seen her last and Byron Dangerfield Grant, Jr., was only now completing his third month in the world.

Like most males, Mr. Hobbs' affection for beings that could neither walk nor talk was more of a tribute to their parents than to their personalities.

It was one of the few real disappointments of his life that his two eldest daughters, instead of settling down comfortably in their home town, had married men without roots, beings apparently destined to spend their lives in remote and unattractive places, all having the common attribute of being inaccessible to grandparents.

There was Susan, for instance, his intelligent, humorous, easygoing oldest daughter who might have married half a dozen men of the type that would lead normal settled lives. Instead, she had unaccountably fallen in love with an inarticulate engineer whose ideal of a home was a place within walking distance of whatever huge and mussy building project he happened to be working on at the moment.

During the five years of their married lives Susan and Stewart Carver, their two beautiful children, a springer spaniel and five barrels of unopened wedding presents, had moved from one dreary dam site to another, surrounded always by either mud or dust and forever within earshot of the clatter of heavy machinery.

The strange thing was that Susan, who in her Vassar days had gone in rather ostentatiously for things cultural, appeared to thrive on this earthy diet. She looked up with loving awe to her taciturn extrovert. She made his ways her ways and prided herself on being able to live anywhere which, from Mr. Hobbs' point of view, was just about where the Carvers lived.

Sometimes Mrs. Hobbs didn't see how Susie stood it—
brought up as she had been. And then there were moments
when she had an uneasy suspicion that perhaps her oldest
daughter actually enjoyed being on her own with no one to
tell her that her housekeeping was on the sloppy side—which
it certainly was—or that young children should lead a regular
life—which Susan's certainly didn't.

To survive in an environment such as the Carvers lived in,
one must become a professional individualist. Susan, with the
naïve brutality of youth, let it be known quite frankly that
she considered her own bringing-up to have been an archaic
mess, whose purpose was not to develop her latent personality,
but solely to erect barriers across socially forbidden paths.
When Peter was born she had informed her mother that she
was about to raise a family along totally different lines—a
family in which the word "don't" was never heard.

When Susan disappeared into the deserts Mr. Hobbs had
pinned his hopes on Jane. No two sisters had ever been more
different. Susan was dark and, in the rare moments when her
face was in repose, rather plain. Jane on the other hand was
beautiful, her beauty crowned with a shock of golden-red hair.
It was a beauty which made strong men grip the edge of
tables when they first beheld it.

Unlike Susan, Jane had never gone to college. This was
partly because everyone knew that she could never get in and
partly because life had been much too full and colorful to
warrant such interruptions.

Perhaps it was just because life had been so bountiful and
so easy that she suddenly lost her heart to a tall, gangly young

man with unruly hair and a mouthful of teeth who, of all things, taught economics at Pendergast University in Indiana. Perhaps it was because, out of all the men who had laid their hearts at her feet, Byron Dangerfield Grant was the first intellectual. Perhaps it was because he was so absent-minded, so lost in his world of ideas, that he seemed unconscious of her beauty. Perhaps it was because the life of Pendergast University was so far removed from anything she had ever known that it contained the challenge for which she had been unconsciously hungering. Whatever the reason, the miracle happened and she married him.

Never having had deep-rooted convictions of her own she had found it easy to adopt her husband's with enthusiasm, insofar as she understood them. She considered Byron's ideas on social philosophy and economic theory as divinely inspired and was prepared to fight her father to the death when he suggested the Kremlin as a more likely source.

At least, as Mrs. Hobbs said, the Grants didn't live in dust bowls and mud holes like the Carvers. And Pendergast wasn't so far away that she couldn't go out once in a while and hang over her grandson's crib with dreamy eyes which refused to see that Byron Dangerfield Grant, Jr., was doomed to look exactly like his father and not at all like his beautiful mother.

"One thing," said Mrs. Hobbs, tapping her pencil against her teeth, "we'll have to buy a play pen."

"Why?" said Mr. Hobbs. "Just why do we have to buy a play pen? We pay an outlandish price for this house just because there are acres and acres of wild land around it for the children to run around in. Then the first thing we do is to drop them into a pen. What is this idea that the modern child mustn't ever play—"

"And there's another thing," said Mrs. Hobbs. "I've tried to borrow two cribs but everybody seems to be using theirs. So I guess we'll have to buy a couple."

"Listen, Peggy, those things cost money. I'm not a maharajah or something. I make my money the hard way and then the government takes it all and you expect me to keep on spending it like water. Besides, what are you going to do with all this stuff when we leave? We'll have to go home in a moving van."

"Do you want the children to sleep on the floor?"

"What would you do if we were very, very poor?" It was a device which he used in such discussions, but Mrs. Hobbs had learned long ago to side-step these philosophical traps.

"I don't know *what* we'd do if we were very, very poor and I don't much care. All I know is the babies have to have two cribs to sleep in."

"Will you help me get some of these things into the house?" called Mrs. Hobbs.

Mr. Hobbs sat up on the couch swing and peered sleepily over the verandah rail. The rear of the sedan was piled to the roof with cartons and packages and the gaping baggage compartment was tied with a rope.

"Good God," said Mr. Hobbs, "where are we going to *put* all this stuff. We ought to have rented a warehouse instead of a summer place. And who in the world is going to pay for it all? Just because three little children decide to go to the seashore—"

"Listen, Rog, don't get so excited. You go all to pieces before you know anything about it. Most of this is basic stuff. Remember, you're going to have ten hungry mouths to feed. Then there were a few things I *had* to get, like an indoor

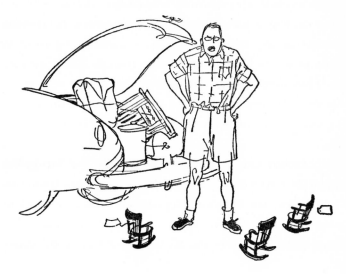

drier and an extra pot for boiling diapers and a bathinette—"

"A what?"

"Oh you know. A thing to bathe the baby in."

"Oh," said Mr. Hobbs. "It sounded like one of those diving jobs Beebe uses."

"Don't try to be sarcastic," said Mrs. Hobbs. "You're not natural when you're sarcastic. That's about all. I had to lay in a lot of baby food—oh yes—and I got a stroller. We had to have *something* to take them out in."

"Are the Carvers and the Grants bringing anything except the children?" asked Mr. Hobbs, but Mrs. Hobbs was burrowing among the packages in the rear of the car.

"Isn't that stupid, Rog. I left the life belts and the curtains at Terrey's store. You'll have to drive back and get them for me. I've got too many other things to do."

"The life belts and the what?" asked Mr. Hobbs.

"Oh darling, I just bought some inexpensive, ready-made curtains for the children's rooms. I couldn't *stand* those ghastly pink and blue things another minute. These are very cute. They have Mother Goose pictures on them."

"I see," said Mr. Hobbs. "By the way do you think we'd have time to repaint the house inside and out before they get here?"

Mrs. Hobbs didn't bother to reply. She was struggling through the screen door with an armful of packages. He untied the rope from the baggage compartment. Inside, jammed in among the packages, were three tiny rocking chairs. He unloaded them carefully and set them in a row on the driveway.

"Listen, Peggy," he called.

Mrs. Hobbs' voice came from somewhere within the house. "Just set everything on the porch and go down to Terrey's before they close. And while you're in town you might pick up a couple of bottles of catsup. We're having canned corned beef hash tonight. I'm too tired to do any cooking."

After driving the entire length of Main Street three times Mr. Hobbs finally found a parking place not too far from

Elwell Terrey's General Store. Miss Haskell, Mr. Terrey's ageless, sexless clerk, met him just inside the door.

"Good morning," she said. "I've seen you around, but I don't think I know your name."

"Good morning," he said. "Hobbs."

"Oh, Mr. Hobbs—Grey Gables. I was wondering what you'd look like. Mr. Terrey and I were talking yesterday about how they'd jacked the price of that old place up this year. I guess when things are prosperous, though, people'll pay anything. I'm glad you dropped in. Mrs. Hobbs was here and left two packages. Wait a minute and I'll get them."

She disappeared through a door in the rear of the store.

Mr. Hobbs strolled past the sports-wear counter and found himself in the toy department. He was examining a circular rubber swimming pool when Miss Haskell returned.

"There you are," she said. "Mrs. Hobbs said you had some grandchildren coming. Those collapsible swimming pools are nice. They've put a terrible price on them, but for those that have the money they're nice. They didn't have contraptions like that when I was a girl, but it seems these modern kids have to be sitting in water all the time and throwing it around. They certainly are nice for that."

"How much are they?" asked Mr. Hobbs.

"I really hate to mention it," said Miss Haskell. "Twenty-four sixty. Seems awful, doesn't it? But I guess everything's that way what with taxes an' one thing an' another. I see you looking at those big rubber horses. Those are nice too if you've got the price. The children like them when they go in bathing. They're handy for them if they get out beyond their depth and can't swim. You know how children are. We've got a fine line of velocipedes, too. Don't know where you're going to ride them around here without getting run over, but the kids go for them."

An hour later Miss Haskell and Mr. Elwell Terrey accompanied Mr. Hobbs to his car. Each carried a double armful of merchandise.

"You're sure going to be a popular grandpa," said Mr. Terrey. "Nothing like grandchildren, though. All the fun and none of the cost, as I say to my wife. Just drop in on them when you feel like it, and leave when you want. Not like with your own children. Well, good-by now. We're certainly much obliged to you. Stop in next week. We've got a new shipment coming in."

"Where in the world have you been, Rog? You don't realize how much there is to do. Now listen, I've got an entirely new plan and it's a wonderful improvement. Instead of having Susan and Stewart in the *downstairs* bedroom where they can't hear the babies I've decided to give them *our* bedroom. I knew you wouldn't mind. If you didn't hate double beds so we could leave our single beds just where they are—but you do and that's that, I suppose. I've taken all the beds apart. All you've got to do is switch around the pieces and the mattresses, put them together again and we're all set. Then I want you to take Peewee's crib out of the room at the head of the stairs and—"

Mr. Hobbs interrupted. "Now look, Peggy. After all this is *my* vacation, too. I'll do anything at all for the kids if it makes any sense, but why in the world I should—"

Mrs. Hobbs was peering through the window of the sedan. "Roger Hobbs, what in the world have you got in that car?"

"Oh, just some little things I thought might be fun," said Mr. Hobbs uncomfortably.

"Fun!" There was a note of hysteria in Mrs. Hobbs' voice. "You talk to me about spending money. How much—"

"Listen, Peggy, why don't we talk about that later. If you've taken all the beds apart I suppose that settles it and we might as well get things shifted around while there's plenty of light. I want to get into a pair of old pants."

He entered the house. Mrs. Hobbs followed him, smiling slightly.

10

It's a philosophy
as much as a sport

The sound of an alarm clock jarred Mr. Hobbs out of a deep sleep. He knew immediately that this was an unusual day, but for the moment he could not recall what was to make it so. According to the clock, it was only six-thirty. He could hear Mrs. Hobbs splashing in the bathroom.

Of course! Where were his wits? This was the day the Carvers arrived. But they weren't due until the twelve-thirty boat.

"What's the idea in getting up in the middle of the night?" he called.

"Because there are about ten thousand things to be done before everyone gets here, that's why. Please don't just lie there in a stupor, Rog. We're never going to get the place ready."

"What's the matter with it right now?"

"If you can't see for yourself there's not much use trying to explain. At least get up so I can make the beds and get breakfast out of the way."

Mr. Hobbs opened his mouth to say something very funny. Then he thought better of it and swung his feet to the floor. Outside the ocean was brilliant in the early sunlight. It was a good day to be alive and, once dressed and fully awake, he went about his chores with a light heart. He liked the early part of the day and each time he was forced by some uncontrollable circumstance to participate in it he resolved to make early rising a part of his routine thereafter.

"Please don't dawdle over your coffee," said Mrs. Hobbs. "You could be *such* a help if you wanted to."

"By doing *what*? You tell me what you want done and I'll do it."

"Well, the living room has to be cleaned up. It's all cluttered with your papers and letters and things. I wish you'd go through them and get rid of what you don't want."

"Why should a man start destroying his private papers just because his grandchildren are coming?" grumbled Mr. Hobbs. "Do you want me to throw away all your knitting, too?"

He collected the offending papers and stuffed them into a drawer. It irked him to be hauled out of bed at six-thirty in the morning to perform this simple task. "What else?" he bawled.

Mrs. Hobbs' voice came faintly from upstairs. "Look around," she said.

He did. For the life of him he didn't see what else could be done to the living room. Did she want him to move all the furniture out on the lawn and beat the rugs? He wandered aimlessly onto the porch. There wasn't a cloud in the sky and a soft, cool breeze from the sea tempered the rays of the morning sun. On a table lay the canvas case containing his surf casting rod.

The back door slammed. He saw Mrs. Hobbs cross the lawn in the direction of the drying yard. He went into the house and reappeared a few minutes later dressed in a pair of bathing trunks, an old flannel shirt and a pair of sneakers with holes in them. He took the casting rod and a tin box from the table and, with an uneasy glance toward the rear of the house, started down the steps.

"Roger Hobbs, where are you going?"

He stopped, feeling like a guilty schoolboy and irritated with himself because of it. "There didn't seem to be anything else to do around here so I thought I'd just go out to the beach for a few minutes," he said apologetically.

"Do you know what time it is? It's almost nine o'clock. If you get down on that beach you'll never be back in time to meet the boat."

"I promise. Good Lord, dear, the boat doesn't come in for hours. Anyway they've got their own car. I don't see why it's so important to meet them at all."

"It *is* important," said Mrs. Hobbs. "It's *very* important. They've never been on the Island before and they have no idea where we live and once you set foot on that beach you're perfectly irresponsible."

"I'll be back," said Mr. Hobbs. "I'll be back at half past eleven."

He stopped in front of the Ogdens' white shingled cottage and sounded his horn. Mrs. Ogden, wearing a red shirtwaist and white shorts, came to the door. "Rather luscious," thought Mr. Hobbs. Aloud he said, "Good morning, Joan. Do you think Jack would want to go up the beach with me for an hour or so?"

"He can't," said Mrs. Ogden decisively. "He's promised to do some things for me around the place."

Mr. Ogden appeared in the doorway behind her. "Hi," he said.

"Hi," said Mr. Hobbs. "I just stopped by to see if you wanted to take your rod and go down to the beach with me for half an hour or so. Joan says you're tied up though."

"Yes, I promised her I'd do some work around the place. I don't see why it can't wait for a while though. Going to be gone long?"

"No. Just down and back," said Mr. Hobbs. "I have to be home right away."

"Wait a minute while I get my rod." Jack Ogden disappeared into the house.

"I hate you," said Mrs. Ogden and let the screen-door slam.

"Spoiled type," thought Mr. Hobbs.

He loved the lonely five-mile stretch of sand where he and Jack Ogden fished. Although it was by far the best beach on the Island, for some reason the land behind it had never been developed. The great dunes gave way to bayberry thickets and these in turn merged into scrub pine, uncut by path or track except in one place known only to a few who didn't mind scratching the sides of their cars on the way in.

The scalloped line of the beach was the battle front where the sea and the land met in endless struggle. It was not a rigid front. Sand bars rose and fell. The dunes were built up through the years, destroyed and built again. In the cosmic sense it was a fluid line. In the observation of mortal man, however, the change was too slight to be observed.

The waves continued to beat gently or to pound savagely against the yielding sands, as they had been doing for thousands of years, occasionally smoothing them out into broad, gentle slopes and at other times piling them up so that they shelved steeply into the curling green depths.

Occasionally a lone walker appeared around a distant point, a black speck at first emerging from the gray spume which fogged the beach at each end. So great were the distances that he seemed scarcely to move. Then he slowly grew to human proportions and just as slowly diminished until, reduced again to a black spot, he disappeared once more into the spume from which he had come, leaving behind a long trail of duck-toed footprints.

As if resentful of this intrusion, land and water declared a momentary armistice and joined forces to eliminate the evidence. The lower tracks were quickly washed out by the waves while the wind poured grain after grain of sand into those higher up until they became shapeless hollows and then disappeared entirely.

The incoming tide used the beach as a repository for all manner of curious things. Like a tireless retriever it laid down its oddly assorted burdens and then rushed back for more—electric light bulbs deposited by the flood tides of August, great timbers brought to the foot of the dunes on the strong shoulders of winter waves, boxes and crates, bits of wood of every size and shape, a suitcase—upended and open—its lining fluttering raggedly in the fresh southwest breeze.

Although most of these objects were man's handiwork they somehow seemed to belong more to the beach than to man once the coarse white sand grains had begun to drift about their lower edges. The suitcase was no longer the property of the sailor who had carried it aboard a coastal steamer months before. The great beam with the rusty spike at one end was no longer a part of the wrecked fishing schooner from which it had been torn. Even the electric light bulbs belonged to and were a part of the beach just as much as the stranded jellyfish and the empty shells of the horseshoe crabs.

On each sandy point colonies of sea gulls drowsed in the August sun. Among the seaweed the sandpipers scurried excitedly, running forward with twinkling legs, stopping to peck, then rushing frantically to the next morsel. Over a deep place beside the point the tern circled and dove, rose, circled and dove again and then disappeared up the beach. In the dry seaweed near the dunes the sand fleas jumped restlessly like bubbles rising from the surface of champagne.

Mr. Hobbs liked to fish with Jack Ogden. Jack was a realistic sort of person who didn't waste time on the amenities.

As soon as they reached the shore he selected his plug and then started off without a word, never stopping to cast until they were separated by at least a quarter of a mile. They would maintain this interval, working slowly down the beach, until the car among the dunes was hidden by intervening points and they were completely alone in a world of sand and sea and sky.

In such a vast setting two men could be good company to one another even when standing a quarter of a mile apart. From Mr. Hobbs' point of view this separation was highly desirable for he was not an expert fisherman. In fact this was the first summer he had ever cast a plug and he wanted no one around to observe the results.

He would watch Jack Ogden carefully as, without apparent effort, the younger man sent his line flying out beyond the spot where the water began to hump up into waves. What was even more amazing was to see him reel it in casually without ever fouling his hooks on unseen rocks.

It was all so easy when Jack Ogden did it. Mr. Hobbs would memorize every motion before carefully lowering the tip of his pole behind him. After many backward glances to be sure that all was in order he would bring the pole over his shoulder with a fine snap of the wrist and watch the plug hopefully as it started upward and seaward.

If it was a good cast, he would become so fascinated by his own skill that he was apt to forget to check the flying line with his thumb just before it struck the water. Then his reel would suddenly become filled with a mess of tangled loops protruding from it in all directions.

At such moments he would glance apprehensively down the beach to see if Ogden had noticed, but the latter was always engaged in a faultless rhythm of casting and reeling.

Mr. Hobbs would then back up to the dry sand where there were old timbers on which one could sit. There he would begin the interminable business of tweaking at the hopelessly tangled line. If he found a good place to sit and the sun was shining it could be a rather pleasant process. In fact if it had not been for his fear that Ogden would look down the beach and behold his ignominy he would just as soon unravel as cast.

Neither of them ever caught a striper anyway. The only living thing that ever emerged from the waves was an occasional unhappy flounder. After a while Mr. Hobbs learned to expect nothing and even resented the flounders as intruders. Given a lonely beach and a high blue sky it really didn't matter much whether or not one caught fish. The important thing was just being there.

Eventually and miraculously the kinks always came out, but casting was full of other pitfalls. For example, no matter how careful he was Mr. Hobbs was apt to leave a loose spot on his line as he wound it back on the reel. On the next cast, the line would start flying out with a fine free whine— then suddenly stop with a jerk which sent the plug plummeting into the waves at his feet. This particular type of mishap used to humiliate him more than any of the others. It was the stuff on which clown humor is based.

The accident which filled him with real dismay, however, was the snag. He would be fishing over a place where Jack

Ogden had been casting not more than fifteen minutes before without the slightest difficulty. But, as Mr. Hobbs reeled in his line slowly and carefully, it would suddenly grow taut.

The practical part of his mind knew immediately that somewhere beneath those tossing waves lay a rock and that one of his hooks had found it. The romantic section, however, always suggested that an enormous striper might well lie at the end of the line, momentarily stunned by the unfamiliar check on its freedom. In the window of Jasper Haskell, the coal and grain dealer of Rock Harbor, was an enormous stuffed striper, a record affair, caught after a titanic struggle by one Anthony V. Montrose of Brockton, Massachusetts, in 1939. As Mr. Hobbs watched the tip of his rod bend toward the straining line the image of this dusty champion always came to his mind, only now he saw a different inscription which read "Caught by Roger Hobbs. Time 5 hours 42 minutes. Weight 62 pounds."

This sort of vicarious pleasure only lasted for a moment, however. He quickly realized that he was the one who was caught and not a fish. Glancing furtively down the beach toward Ogden he would lower the tip of his rod and pull as hard as he dared, hoping against hope that this was just a small stone which he could dislodge or a clump of seaweed.

Apparently, however, he had become fouled up with the lip of the continental shelf. Letting out line he would walk down the beach and try yanking at it from an angle. Then he would walk in the opposite direction and pull again without result. Finally he would find himself raging back and forth

like a caged animal pulling frantically on the line at the end
of each run.

These unfortunate entanglements never seemed to happen in the placid spots where the beach sloped gently away
into gradually deepening water and friendly little waves
broke gently against one's knees. Instead they occurred in-

variably where, a few feet out, the sand fell off steeply to
unknown depths. At the edge of the shelf the rollers reared
like angry dragons, exposing for a moment the cruel dark
green sheen of their undersides, before they came crashing
down on the shifting sand and spent themselves in
white foam around Mr. Hobbs' ankles.

Exhausted with running back and forth he would raise
the tip of the rod as high as possible in an attempt to discover

how far out his hook was snagged. It couldn't be more than thirty feet away, but to go after it would involve stepping off that sandy shelf into the curling waves and then following the line through the tumbling waters to the bottom.

At such moments he would glance uncertainly at Ogden, fishing rhythmically down the beach. Ogden would know what to do. Were he here he would have the hook free in an instant and hand the rod back with a good-natured grin. To hell with Ogden.

Mr. Hobbs would begin, at this point, to give serious thought to taking the plunge. If he ever succeeded in reaching the hook the tossing waves would probably imbed it in his eye or his ear and leave him thrashing around in the surf like one of his own fish. What fish?

It would make an interesting item for the local paper. The Associated Press might even pick it up. "Summer fisherman has strange accident. While diving beneath the waves—" He amended the article. "While diving beneath giant waves to loosen his hook Surffisherman Roger Hobbs of Grey Gables was impaled by the barb—" He changed it again. "Strange disappearance of Roger Hobbs, well-known businessman and sportsman. While surf casting with John Ogden of the Rock Harbor summer colony, Mr. Hobbs—"

Absorbed in these morbid but fascinating thoughts he had lowered the tip of his rod. Now as he raised it for a final tug he found the line suddenly slack. He reeled it in frantically and a moment later the dreaded hooks were washing about harmlessly at his feet. Ogden was walking toward him, his rod over his shoulder.

It was time to quit. No use casting again and risking another snag. Mr. Hobbs walked back to the dunes and sat down on a bleaching timber. The sun seemed suddenly to shine more warmly, the blue water seemed more friendly and Mr. Hobbs noted with surprise that, during the last few minutes, the waves had subsided into inconsequential little rollers that a child could have handled.

Jack Ogden sat down wearily beside him. "Get anything?"

"Not a thing. How about you?"

"Not a nibble. Wonderful morning though."

"Wasn't it?" said Mr. Hobbs.

Together they walked back to the car. "I've got to begin thinking of the time," said Mr. Hobbs. "We're meeting that twelve-thirty boat. Couple of grandchildren pulling in."

He reached into the tin tackle box for his wrist watch. It was a quarter to one.

11

The making of a patriarch

Mr. Hobbs was in the doghouse.

He didn't need to be told officially. The emptiness and immaculate neatness of Grey Gables pronounced its silent verdict. The old house seemed to say reproachfully, "At least there was *someone* here who didn't forget. At least there was *someone* who worked tirelessly to put me in proper order while you splashed around childishly trying to catch something that wasn't there—*and you knew it.*"

Filled with misery and self-pity he sat down in the living room. For the first time he noticed a piece of paper pinned to the mantel. He took it down apprehensively. It had been scrawled by Mrs. Hobbs in what, from all visual evidence, must have been a moment of considerable emotional tension.

I was never so mad in my life. First you go off with that fool Ogden leaving all the work to me. Then you forget to come home, leaving me without a car. [It was the first time Mr. Hobbs had thought of this complication.] Mary Ogden is taking me to the boat. For pity's sake, if it ever occurs to you to come home, stay at the house. See there's plenty of hot water if that isn't asking too much and *don't use the clean towels.*

Mr. Hobbs sighed remorsefully. The trouble with surf casting was that it took you to places where time was an artificial concept and even the meaningless recordings of a wrist watch were unavailable as all such gadgets had to be left in the tackle box. But try to explain things like that to a woman!

He went out to the kitchen to find something to eat. The icebox was crammed with mysterious objects, wrapped neatly in wax paper. He shut the door without further exploration and made himself a peanut butter sandwich moistened with catsup. He despised peanut butter and catsup sandwiches, but they were the only two ingredients in the kitchen which he felt safe in using at the moment.

He wandered back to the living room. Everything had such a scrubbed and ordered look that he hardly recognized the place. All extraneous objects had disappeared—probably forever, he thought resentfully, noting several personal belongings which were missing. Their places had been taken by vases of wild flowers and there were great bunches of bayberry at each end of the usually littered mantel.

He went upstairs to check the hot-water heater, wash and change his clothes. In the bathroom all the workaday towels and washcloths had been replaced by magnificent monogrammed affairs with the fat look which he had learned to associate with guest towels.

He washed his hands and dried them on a handful of Mrs. Hobbs' paper handkerchiefs. Then he went to his bedroom to dress. The bureau drawers were all empty and lined with fresh pink paper. He remembered that he and Mrs. Hobbs had moved to the downstairs bedroom.

He eventually found an old pair of slacks which he put on and went down to the pumphouse. Might as well fill the tanks and be on the safe side. The pumphouse was his undisputed domain. Just to look out over the water, across the tops of the bayberry bushes, made him feel better immediately.

He sat down on a broken box and let his mind wander over the weeks which lay ahead. It was curious how the relationship of everything seemed to shift the moment grandchildren came on the scene. Susan and Jane, for instance, suddenly ceased to be his "children" and became his "married daughters."

The change-over was a subtle one, but it was none the less real. With motherhood they had acquired new insights, a new wisdom which made them almost strangers, although outwardly they were the same. Mr. Hobbs found himself slightly afraid of them and he instinctively knew that from now on this would always be so.

The change was not confined to Susan and Jane. He had noted it in Peggy also, although in her case it was more difficult for him to put his finger on just what it was. She was probably living the days of her early married life over again through her grandchildren. The difference was that this was a vicarious experience which she could go through alone and unaided. It was an emotional adventure entailing no real responsibility—an adventure in which the old parental team played no necessary part.

Mr. Hobbs rose impatiently. In a few minutes he'd be feeling sorry for himself. The forgotten grandfather! Nuts! He walked rapidly up the hill. As he reached the top the Ogdens' car turned into the drive followed by a mud-encrusted station wagon.

The inside of the latter vehicle was piled to the roof with suitcases and cartons between which odd bits of clothing and gear had been stuffed like mortar until a semi-solid mass had been created. Young Peter Carver hung from one of the middle windows, glumly surveying the unfolding prospect. Peewee sat on a hanging seat between her parents. As the car came to a halt she began to scream.

The front door of the station wagon flew open. Susan and a large springer spaniel came bounding out together. Susan threw herself into her father's arms. "Pops!"

He kissed her—then, his hands on her shoulders, he pushed her away gently so that he could look at her. "Darling, you're wonderful. Gosh, I'm glad to see you."

"*You've* certainly been a big help," said Mrs. Hobbs. His happiness faded like a mirage. He was shaking hands with his big son-in-law, however, and the need for rebuttal was postponed.

"Gracious," said Mrs. Hobbs. "I didn't know you were

bringing a *dog*." The springer, who had been running in circles and barking furiously, had suddenly begun to throw himself on Mrs. Hobbs with joyful yelps.

"Of *course*, Mother. That's Rumpus. We never go *anywhere* without Rumpus. Peter, don't you see Bompa. Get out and give him a big bear hug."

"I don't want to," said Peter, moving to the other side of the station wagon. "I don't like this place. I want to go home."

"But Peter, darling, this is Bompa that you've talked about so much. Don't you like Bompa?"

"No," cried Peter. He stuck his fists in his eyes and began to howl.

"He's tired," said Susan.

"Of course he is—poor little thing. For heaven's sake, Roger, leave him alone and help Stewart unload the car."

"They'll be all right when they get some food in them and have a nap. I'll take Peewee and Peter and leave you and Stew to handle the junk, Pops. I wouldn't say anything to Peter right now."

She pulled Peewee out of the hanging seat and entered the house, followed by Mrs. Hobbs dragging Peter. It was not just the way Mr. Hobbs had planned it. Mrs. Ogden waved to no one in particular and drove away. Mr. Hobbs joined his son-in-law at the back of the station wagon feeling suddenly shy and awkward.

"Well, Stew," he said heartily. "Good to see you."

"Good to see *you*, sir." That was it. This constant use of the word "sir." How could you ever be at ease with someone who was always calling you "sir."

"How are things out in Los Alamos?" It was a silly question.

"Oh, fine, fine, sir. I hope everything's fine with you." It was an equally silly answer.

"Have a hard trip?"

"Oh no sir. Only four nights on the road. We drive pretty fast and the kids are used to it. Peter always throws up a good deal the first day out. Then he settles into the groove. He's a good little traveler."

"I see," said Mr. Hobbs. He was dismayed to find that they had reached the end of their conversational rope in forty seconds flat with ten days to go. A mountain of baggage was beginning to accumulate on the driveway.

"Stew." It was Susan at the front door. "Will you bring in the carton with the children's things in it so I can get their supper started and get them to bed?"

Stewart Carver selected a bulging carton. "Excuse me, sir. I'll be right back."

"Don't hurry," said Mr. Hobbs.

"Yes sir," said Stewart and staggered up the steps with his burden.

Methodically and grimly Mr. Hobbs unloaded the dusty contents of the station wagon, down to the last broken plastic toy—the last discarded paper handkerchief. The result lay about him on the driveway and lawn. It looked more like wreckage than baggage. Stewart did not return.

Well, there was no use standing here staring at the stuff. He picked up two suitcases and carried them up to the second floor.

On his way back to the car he stuck his head in the kitchen door. Mrs. Hobbs waved him away. "For goodness' sake don't come in here and add more confusion. Just get their things upstairs so we can get these children to bed."

Slowly, like the builders of the pyramids, he toiled upward with his burdens. No one paid any attention to him or told him what went where, so he piled everything in a huge mound at the head of the stairs.

With each trip he felt his strength ebbing, his heart pounding faster and faster. Each time he revolved through the screen door, clutching a great carton or a suitcase, the thought occurred to him that this might be his last load. He wondered how it would feel. "Suddenly Mr. Hobbs' face turned ashen white. He spun around and pitched headlong down the steep stairs to lie unnoticed at the bottom."

The vision upset him so that he did not attempt to bring up the smaller packages and loose things but merely piled them in the immaculate living room wherever he could find a place.

Several hours later Mr. Hobbs stood before the living-room table thoughtfully agitating a shakerful of martinis. He stood because there was no place to sit down. The room was a shambles. Every table and chair was covered with half-opened packages and the floor was so littered with cartons, wrapping paper, toys, clothes, sneakers, battered picture books and other oddments of family life that it was with difficulty he made his way round the room to distribute the contents of the shaker.

Susan sat curled up on the sofa, her bare feet protruding from the edges of a striped beach skirt. Mr. Hobbs decided she must have Moslem blood in her. His oldest daughter had never been able to keep a pair of shoes on her feet once she crossed a threshold and apparently she did not own a pair of stockings.

"I must say I think drinking cocktails in bare feet is about the sloppiest performance—" he began.

"*Pops!* What in the world has drinking a cocktail got to do with whether you're barefooted or wearing rubber boots? Why do you get yourself so worked up by a lot of fuzzy—"

"Because," said Mr. Hobbs. "There are some things that—"

"Now listen, Roger. This is the first night. Stop fussing." Mrs. Hobbs' voice indicated that if they could get through this initial period she could cope with future violence.

Susan, quite unperturbed by the incident, sipped a martini and watched Peter with loving eyes. He was engaged in removing objects from the tables and hurling them to the floor.

"Look," said Mr. Hobbs, as a heavy glass ashtray went down with a crash but miraculously did not break. "This stuff isn't mine. I have to pay for the pieces. Lay off it, Peter. *Hey!*" He caught a tottering lamp and pushed it to the back of the table.

Peter looked at him with hostile eyes and reached for a cigarette box. Mr. Hobbs set down the shaker and approached him menacingly. "Now look here, young fellow. I told you to lay off that. And when I tell you something I mean it. Now listen to me. I don't want you to touch *anything-on-those-tables*. Do you understand?"

For a moment Peter stared at Mr. Hobbs in astonishment. Then his face became contorted with anguish and he ran sobbing to his mother.

"For goodness' sake, Roger. What's the matter with you?" said Mrs. Hobbs.

Susan looked troubled. "I hate to say this, Pops, 'cause of course it's your house and everything, but Stew and I don't believe in that sort of thing. We never say 'no' to either of the children. All the modern psychologists agree it's the only way to bring up kids without neuroses. If they're doing something you don't want them to do, substitute something else. All these ashtrays and things we'll just pile up on the mantel."

She began to remove objects from the table. The fire irons came down with a crash around Peewee.

Susan pulled her out from under them. "That's all right. She's not hurt. Just scared. Here, dear, you can play with them now."

Mr. Hobbs refilled his glass and drank it off quickly.

"Everybody go on to bed," said Mr. Hobbs. "I'll put this stuff out in the kitchen. Then I'll take Rumpus out. I need a breath of air."

He carried half a dozen empty ginger ale bottles and several glasses into the kitchen. By the time he had washed the glasses and put them away and put the bottles outside everyone had disappeared.

Everyone, that is, except Rumpus, who lay on the sofa, his nose between his paws. His eyes followed Mr. Hobbs suspiciously as the latter moved about the room.

"Come on, boy," said Mr. Hobbs in his best coaxing voice. Rumpus did not remove his nose from his paws and continued to stare coldly.

"Up we come, boy," said Mr. Hobbs in his heartiest Boy Scout manner. He approached with outstretched hand. Rumpus gave out a low, businesslike growl.

Mr. Hobbs pulled the fire tongs from under a chair where Peewee had cached them. "Get off that sofa, you bastard," he said in a choked voice. Rumpus glanced at the upraised fire tongs, slid off the sofa and under it. Mr. Hobbs turned off the lights.

Susan's voice called down to him through her closed door. "Pops, you didn't forget to take Rumpus out?"

"No," said Mr. Hobbs. "Good night, Bunny."

It was a long time since he had called her that.

"Good night, Pops."

12

Interlude

Mr. Hobbs sat in Sidney Bollivar's barbershop reading a six-weeks-old copy of *Look*. Through the broad front window Mr. Bollivar and his customers had an unobstructed view of what went on in Rock Harbor during the course of the working day. At the moment the mid-morning traffic inched its way along the sun-drenched street, while on the sidewalk outside the window pedestrians bobbed past, singly or in groups, each wearing his or her concept of a summer costume. The faces were pale or lobster red or bronzed, indicating how long they had been on the Island. The old-timers were bare-headed. The newcomers, more cautious, were protected from the noonday sun by every conceivable shape of cap or hat ever fashioned from cloth or straw.

Mr. Bollivar was working on a small boy who had been raised to scissors level by placing a box on the barber's chair. His assistant, a swarthy young man, whose enormous mop of unruly hair indicated that he did not fully believe in his trade, was working on a fat man devoid of hair except for a narrow band connecting the back of his ears. This lack of material, however, did not deter the swarthy young man for a moment. His shears snipped like a miniature mowing machine, occasionally making contact with a stray hair raised by the comb.

Every few minutes the screen door opened and a prospective customer entered. Each one allowed the door to shut itself, unchecked, which it did with a noise like a pistol shot. "How many ahead?"

"Just these two gentlemen and Mrs. Mowrie is bringing in the twins in about half an hour. It'll only be a few minutes."

"O.K. I'll be back later." Again the door would slam. Although Mr. Hobbs braced himself each time it always made him wince.

Mr. Bollivar maintained a steady flow of conversation while he worked. It made no difference to him that the two waiting men were buried in their magazines or that the child in his chair could not understand or that the fat man in the next chair was dozing. His talk was not directed at anyone. It was the Song of the Shears. It flowed from him like a peaceful river whose source is unknown and whose destination is immaterial.

In spite of appearances, however, his audience was not entirely inattentive. Although Mr. Hobbs continued to turn the dog-eared pages of *Look* he had been under the hypnotic spell of Mr. Bollivar's voice since entering the shop. In fact had he been a cat he would have purred. His hair really did not need cutting very badly but he found these visits to Mr. Bollivar soothing to nerves chafed by the turmoil in which he now lived. Had he known it he came to Mr. Bollivar for therapy rather than tonsure.

"I've got photographs in that book under the table to prove it," Mr. Bollivar was saying. "You could look from this window right down to the harbor and like as not you'd have seen a corner of the Mansion House. There won't be anything like the Mansion House again. They don't build 'em like that now. There wasn't a stick left of it. Nobody ever found out how it come to get started—"

Mr. Hobbs turned a page. The voice faded from his consciousness and his mind traveled back to Grey Gables. The Grants had arrived two days after the Carvers—his beautiful Jane, her far from beautiful husband, their three-months-old son, Byron Dangerfield, Jr., and Merrylegs, a melancholy cocker.

He'd been glad to see Jane—glad and puzzled. It had always puzzled him, this infatuation of his red-haired daughter for the lanky economist. How did a girl like Jane *live* in a place like Pendergast—without friends and surrounded by a lot of intellectuals who, in Mr. Hobbs' opinion, were either old fuddy-duddies or budding fellow travelers. In his off-the-record talks with Mrs. Hobbs he had given the match six months.

But considerably over a year had passed and instead of showing disillusionment Jane gave every evidence of being more and more in love with her new life and her brilliant husband.

"My wife and I were living over on the Mainland that winter," said Mr. Bollivar, floating back into the picture. "I was working for a man in Harborport. I can't just recollect his name. It'll come to me in a minute. It wasn't Granger and it wasn't Snyder. I find if you don't try too hard it'll pop up before long. I had a grandmother—"

Another thing that puzzled Mr. Hobbs was that Jane, who used to be such a heedless, fun-loving sort of person, now snapped up all these doctrines and schools-of-thought that Byron fed her like a trout at sunrise. Even Byron's absent-mindedness, a quality which she had always despised in men, appeared in him as something to be cherished and only brought out her mother tenderness.

The arrival of Byron Dangerfield, Jr., three months previously seemed to have filled her cup of happiness to overflowing. Already she was beginning to talk about "trying to have another," a phrase which Mr. Hobbs considered inelegant and immodest. It was hard for him to understand how the Grants could afford *one* child on their income, to say nothing of two—but that was the way these modern kids were. They married while they were in school and then wanted a flock of babies regardless of money or prospects. Women had certainly changed since his time.

"My wife wasn't well that winter," Mr. Bollivar was saying. "She couldn't hold anything on her stomach. I finally took her to Dr. Tinker over in Harborport—some name for a doctor, eh? First he thought it was her gall bladder and then he thought it might be her spleen. Her mother had trouble with her spleen—"

Mr. Hobbs' mind grew bored and wandered back to his family. He began to contrast the Carvers and the Grants. Susan and Stew, for instance, had an easygoing philosophy which carried them confidently from one day to the next. They did not believe in discipline for their children and they were not too insistent upon it for themselves. Money to the Carvers was something to be spent with a deep conviction that it would be replaced, from some source, before more was needed.

Life to the Grants, on the other hand, was a serious affair. Byron Grant thought of it always with a capital L. To him it had a purpose and it was his responsibility to help Destiny achieve it. He was an idealist who wouldn't be downed by history or the law of probabilities.

Like many intellectual idealists whose anxiety about man's ills eventually bring on a mild case of socialism, Byron Grant had an irrational respect for money. Although his income was probably not half so large as that of his engineer brother-in-law, the Grants undoubtedly had saved four times as much as the Carvers in their first year of married life. From a girl who had never given a thought to such matters, Jane Grant had become a tyrant of household economics and, although

Mr. Hobbs suspected that she did it by starving her husband, he had to admit she always had a bank account.

The front door slammed behind a stout woman in shorts who was wearing a straw cap with a peak almost a foot long. A small boy peered sulkily from behind her. "How many ahead?" she asked belligerently.

"Just these two gentlemen and the Mowrie twins."

"I saw the Mowrie twins driving toward Long Beach fifteen minutes ago. Work him in. Johnnie, you stay here. Mr. Bollivar will work you in. Here—look at these." She removed all the remaining magazines from the table and deposited them in Johnnie's lap. "I'll be back with the car in half an hour. Don't do what you did to him last time." The screen door banged behind her.

Mr. Bollivar shook the hair out of the apron and tucked it around Mr. Hobbs' neck. "Yes sir," he said. "There's more and more holds their scallops off the market every year." Mr. Hobbs interrupted.

"Trim it up pretty well along the sides and back," he said, "but leave it a little long at the corners or it sticks out."

"I know," said Mr. Bollivar impatiently. "Reg'lar haircut. You're out at Grey Gables, aren't you? Beautiful out there. Beautiful. It would be a little quiet for me. My wife would like it. She likes things quiet. She's a nervous type. I remember one time my brother-in-law an' his wife came over for two weeks with their three kids. Well sir, it was a riot. They took the place apart. Bedlam from morning to night. Broke everything breakable. I didn't mind. I always say you can't take it with you. Like to have killed my wife though. Gave her acute gastritis—"

"What were you saying about scallops?" asked Mr. Hobbs.

It was noon when he left the barbershop. Only the totally deaf could be unaware of the noon hour in Rock Harbor as it was publicized each day by an electric siren over the Police Station. When the wind was right its brazen note could be heard at Grey Gables.

It was the hour when the summer residents of Rock Harbor were seized by a common impulse to appear on the streets and particularly on Main Street. From one end of its brief course to the other its west curb was lined with the parked cars of shoppers. This left only a narrow lane for those that moved—or at least for those who wanted to move.

Outside the A & P congestion reached its climax and the traffic jam went from bad to hopeless. On the sidewalk harassed mothers, herding young and clutching crumpled lists, milled like a disturbed colony of ants. Store boys in long white coats, also crumpled, staggered through the traffic with huge cartons, blindly and unharmed, a testimony to faith and good brakes.

As they stowed their burdens on the back seats of the parked cars, other frustrated mothers who had been circling the village for half an hour looking for a place to park jolted to a sudden stop and waited for the space that seemed to be in the making. Main Street jolted to a halt behind them.

It was hard to get into these spaces and it was almost as difficult to get out. With the back seat filled with cartons,

cutting off all rear vision, with children standing on the front seat, cutting off all vision to the right, and with three inches leeway front and back, the frustrated driver, her ordinarily pert face set in grim lines, would start to batter her way out. Turn the wheel, then forward—crash, turn the wheel, then reverse—crash. Far up the street a protesting horn sounded then lapsed into discouraged silence.

Turn the wheel, crash. Turn the wheel, then reverse, the right rear tire dented against the curb. Progress! Turn, crash. Turn, crash. Free at last. That final noise was not a crash. It sounded more like metal *rubbing* against metal. Ah well, what's a car for but to enjoy?

This meant no freedom for the mother waiting for the vacant place. Her ordeal was just beginning. She had never been any good at backing into places anyway and five minutes later she had jammed her car between the curb and the car ahead so that a bulldozer could not have moved it in either direction. At that point she would abandon it in a panic, leaving its left front mudguard sticking out a foot into the traffic.

The dammed-up stream, released, flowed again, though sluggishly. Moving against its current the sub-teen youth of Rock Harbor forced its perilous way on bicycles between the east curb and the slowly moving fenders. It couldn't be said that they rode. Their left foot was carried on the pedal, their right on the high curb. Progress was made by pushing with the right foot—a kind of kiddie car technique.

On the sidewalks the remainder of the population of Rock Harbor moved ceaselessly on their mysterious journeyings— sun-baked young mothers in Brooks Brothers shorts, clutch-

ing their purses and dragging their unwilling offspring home
for lunch—middle-aged men in shorts and blue linen coats
—dowagers, colorful as Venetian fishing boats—sightseers,
honeymooners, natives, all going somewhere or at least looking as if they were, carrying on conversations with friends
across the street or in passing cars, wandering into stores, wandering out again, hanging around the paper store waiting
for the *New York Times* and *Tribune* that were due on the
noon boat—restless, sunburned people, most of whom had
been so active for eleven months that it was difficult for
them to be anything but active now even though there was
neither need nor cause.

In spite of their restlessness they had undergone one basic
change. The self-created delays and confusion which surrounded them did not upset them as they would have in other
surroundings. For eleven months of the year this was the
caringest crowd in the world. Now nobody cared.

Nobody cared if it took five minutes or twenty to travel
the half mile that was Main Street. Nobody cared if the car
ahead stopped suddenly so that the driver might tell her
friend, who at the moment was moodily poking melons in
front of a grocery store, that she and Jack would adore to
come and what time. Nobody cared if they moved or stood
still. As long as they were in the stream, nobody cared.

Mr. Hobbs found his car wedged between two others.
By the time he had disentangled it and worked his way out
of town the spell which Mr. Bollivar had thrown over him
had disappeared like dew under the morning sun.

13

It takes organization

The kitchen had become the hub around which the life of the Hobbs family revolved.

It had not been built to accommodate large groups, particularly when each individual member was working on a different project. Kitchen engineers would have described it as having a low congestion point. As a result it was a scene of turmoil from early morning until late at night— a swarming, through which people moved by shoving and pushing and where they obtained what they wanted by reaching over the bent bodies of others.

A constant stream of sound flowed from it to the living room. It was made up of conversation, argument, protest, denunciation and occasional cries of anguish followed by a crash. Mr. Hobbs, seated in the living room, would stir uneasily, but experience had taught him that when nothing could be done it was best to do nothing.

Feeding ten people was bad enough, but in this instance each age group appeared to be eating on a different time schedule. As a result while one meal was being eaten preparations for another were under way. The endlessness of it all was most depressing to Mr. Hobbs. To make things more complicated Jane kept taking over the entire stove periodically for the boiling of diapers and the sterilizing of bottles —a combination which Mr. Hobbs considered revolting, Mrs. Hobbs highly inconvenient and Susan entirely unnecessary if Jane would use a diaper service like a normal person.

The confusion, however, had not been brought about by lack of planning. For weeks Mrs. Hobbs had been reminding

Mr. Hobbs, somewhat severely as if he were the potential root of the trouble, that with such a big household, organization was everything. For instance, she had told him that she proposed to get up each morning a little before the others and put the coffee on. It always seemed to Mr. Hobbs that if any early rising was called for it was Mrs. Hobbs who did it. Why, he wanted to know, couldn't one of the children get up instead of lying in bed with sheets over their faces? Because, Mrs. Hobbs had said, they needed the rest. That was her standard answer. Why they needed it Mr. Hobbs had never been able to discover.

In any event if he would please let her run these matters it would be much simpler. As she was trying to tell him, she would get up first and put the coffee on. After that she and

one of the girls would cook breakfast. Everyone else would sit quietly at the table and there would be no confusion.

It was a good idea. The only hitch was that it did not work. Susan and Jane were so engrossed with the feeding of their young that they were scarcely conscious of breakfast as a meal for themselves. Stewart and Byron were too full of early morning cheerio (and much too hungry) to wait for anyone to cook for them. The little kitchen quickly became a milling confusion in which people popped bread into the oven and went away, other people pulled out the cinders, popped in fresh bread and went away, dogs sniffed in garbage pails and were ejected yelping through the back door, children were trampled underfoot—and, like bubbles through the basic uproar, rose a stream of unnoted remarks. "Mother, isn't there any more Brillo?" "Will *somebody* watch my egg?" "My God, the toast." "Hasn't *anyone* seen Peter's bib?" Lack of response was something that even the speakers seemed to take for granted.

Mr. Hobbs found it most unrestful.

He was the only one who obeyed instructions and sat quietly at the table, only getting up occasionally to let in the dogs who always seemed to be whining for admission at the front door. He couldn't figure out where they kept coming from but, on the other hand, he couldn't stand whining dogs. By sitting quietly and saying nothing he found that eventually one of the girls placed his coffee and eggs before him. That was a satisfying thing about daughters. They had an instinctive maternal feeling for fathers which was a handy characteristic if one just sat quietly looking a bit helpless, and let it operate.

The life of the table came and went. People sat down, ate a mouthful and hurried back to the kitchen. Mr. Hobbs sat at one end, outwardly impervious to the commotion—which was equally impervious to him.

Mrs. Hobbs ate before the others so that she could devote herself to the logistical problem of cleaning things up in the kitchen fast enough to make room for new materials at a sink which had never been engineered for ten people.

Peter and Peewee were placed at the opposite end of the table from Mr. Hobbs although why Susan troubled to put them there he could not understand in view of the fact that neither of them ate anything. He had been brought up on the myth that children were always hungry, but apparently the modern generation took no nourishment until it was well along in years.

It seemed to be Susan's chief concern to keep Peewee supplied with table silver, ashtrays, broken toys, kitchen utensils, assorted stones, sea shells or whatever else might come to hand. Peewee tested each object by crashing it against the tray of her high chair after which, if it failed to break she threw it to the floor in disgust.

Occasionally, probably because this was supposed to be a meal, Susan introduced a bit of toast or bacon into the picture. These diversions Peewee consigned to the floor immediately without even testing them against the tray.

"I should think she'd get more of a kick out of the glass and china. They break easier," suggested Mr. Hobbs. At that moment Peewee managed to get her hands on the egg timer. She raised it high above her head enjoying to the full the blissful instant before total demolition.

"Goddamn it, stop that," yelled Mr. Hobbs, springing from his chair. "That's the egg timer." Peewee eyed him with amazement as Mr. Hobbs snatched it away. Then her face contorted and she began to howl. Susan came running.

"Dad, what in the world are you doing to her? Oh you poor little dear! Did naughty Bompa scare you to death?"

Mrs. Hobbs abandoned her sink. "For pity's sake, Roger. What *are* you trying to do to the child. I heard you swear at her. You ought to be *ashamed* of yourself."

"She was trying to smash the egg timer," mumbled Mr. Hobbs, but Susan had picked Peewee up and was walking with her up and down the living room. He had already been forgotten.

Peter's place was at Susan's other side. He was also on a hunger strike, but his approach was more mature than Peewee's. With hands clenching the seat of his chair, he scowled at Mr. Hobbs over an untouched plate of bacon and eggs, a full glass of milk and a glass of orange juice, which he had partially disposed of through spillage.

Susan paid no attention. Mr. Hobbs controlled himself as long as possible. Eventually he came to the breaking point. "Listen, Susan. Are you going to sit there and watch that child starve himself to death? I haven't seen him eat for two days."

Peter's eyes brightened with anticipation. The lines of his mouth curved downward more sharply. Mrs. Hobbs, her ears always alerted for trouble, called from the kitchen. "Now Roger, don't *you* get into that. You let Susan bring up her children *her* way."

"That's O.K. with me," said Mr. Hobbs. "All I want to do

is keep them from starving to death on the premises." Susan, unperturbed, rose, removed the unbroken eggs, the untasted milk and the unspilled orange juice and carried them into the kitchen. An expression of pain came into Mr. Hobbs' face as he heard the eggs being scraped into the garbage pail. If he had only visualized the situation he might have raised some kind of livestock on this unexpected by-product.

Peter slid from his chair and stood beside his grandfather. "Take off my bib," he demanded.

The sound of the wasted eggs was still in Mr. Hobbs' ears. "Look here, young fellow, you say 'please' to me when you want me to do something. And let me tell you something else. Eggs and bacon and milk cost money. Don't you know there are millions of boys in this world that would give their shirts for that breakfast? You'd eat it if you were *my* child, by gosh. You'd eat it or you'd go to your room and stay there."

"Pops, will you *please!*" It was too late. Peter, having finally succeeded in creating the crisis for which he had been yearning, burst into anguished cries.

Mrs. Hobbs stuck her head into the living room. "I hope you're satisfied," she said.

"As a matter of fact, sir, I think you're absolutely right," said Byron Grant, extinguishing a cigarette in his coffee cup.

"Well, that's *your* opinion," said Stewart Carver, relighting his pipe carefully. "Susan and I just happen to have different ideas."

Jane Grant's modulated voice from the kitchen: "I think I hear Byron, dear. Will you run up and see if he needs changing? I'm doing the formula."

Susan's voice from the porch. "For heaven's sake, darling,

stick to it and get your precious diapers boiled before I have
to cook Peter's lunch."

"Wasted effort," shouted Mr. Hobbs. "Why cook it? It's
easier to throw it away raw."

Before this avalanche of people had descended on him Mr.
Hobbs had also made careful plans for handling his end of the
household duties. Mrs. Hobbs had said that one thing she
couldn't stand was a lot of men bumbling around the kitchen,
a sentiment which aroused no opposition from Mr. Hobbs.
And so, by mutual consent, the chores and the housecleaning
had become his responsibility.

He spent an evening drawing up a neat schedule which he
tacked up conspicuously by the kitchen door. Stew Carver
was to take care of the pump. That would show how good an
engineer he was, thought Mr. Hobbs grimly. Stew was also
assigned to the garbage and the bottle and can details. Byron
Grant was the emptier of scrap baskets, tender of the incinerator and general grounds keeper.

Kate was so utterly hopeless in the kitchen that Mrs. Hobbs
had donated her also to Mr. Hobbs' team. He appointed her
cleaner of the upstairs quarters and remover of sand from
the front stairs.

For himself he retained the portfolio of Minister of the
Living Room. Basically he was a neat man. Chaos distressed
him. By taking over the living room he could be assured that,
once a day at least, it would be in order.

The early morning picture was discouraging. Every inch
of space was covered by broken toys, incomplete decks of

cards, dog-eared magazines, half-finished letters, capless fountain pens, half-empty packages of cigarettes, letters and postcards from friends, pipes, books, knitting, mending, photographs and all the rest of the confetti of living which is inevitably dropped by a group of people in the course of a day.

It would have been a problem what to do with it all had
it not been for an empty chest of drawers at one end of the
room. He allocated a half drawer to each adult and the top
drawer for unidentified objects. Each morning he collected all
the flotsam on top of the chest and sorted it, item by item,
into its proper place like a postmaster.

It was, of course, an unwarranted infringement of private
rights and audibly regarded as such by everyone, but the daily
miracle of creating order out of confusion brought peace to
his soul and he went about his work heedless of protests.

He also found that, in the course of these morning round-
ups, lost personal articles had a way of turning up. A missing pair of glasses from under the sofa, a pipe stowed away
in a battered trailer truck or a fountain pen being used as a
bookmark.

The broken toys, shells and colored stones presented another problem until it occurred to him to use the big round
woodbasket as a dump for these juvenile collections. Unlike
their elders, neither Peter nor Peewee regarded this as a
violation of their privacy. On the contrary they were enthusi-
astic about the whole idea and the happiest moment of their
day was when Mr. Hobbs had finished his morning cleanup
and they could spill the contents of the big basket in an allur-
ing pile on the living-room floor.

It was a well-thought-out system, but, like Mrs. Hobbs' organizational plans, it did not work. Stewart and Byron were full of good will. Their spirit of co-operation was 100 per cent. Both of them, however, believed that one of their inalienable privileges was to sit on the rail of the porch and smoke for an undetermined time after breakfast.

No references to their responsibilities which Mr. Hobbs might make through the open windows of the living room

were broad enough or insulting enough to dislodge them. Concentrated on their unending arguments they were oblivious to time, which slipped serenely by while from the kitchen complaints about overflowing garbage pails and scrap baskets and declining water pressure became steadily louder.

Eventually, yielding to a fate over which he seemed to have no control, Mr. Hobbs would find himself at the pump-house or watching the writhings of burning cartons or relieving his feelings by throwing empty bottles at the conical rock.

When his sons-in-law saw him returning from these expeditions they were genuinely distressed. If only he would give them a moment to relax after breakfast all these things would be cared for. This was *his* vacation. He should not be asked to lift a finger.

They meant it. Mr. Hobbs knew that. They were good boys, his sons-in-law. He went upstairs to inspect Kate's department. Her bedroom door was still closed. Getting a broom and dust pan from the hall closet he swept around the edges of the rugs, working quietly so as not to wake her.

14

Evening

Although no one had suggested otherwise, Mr. Hobbs declared fiercely at the beginning of his vacation that his evenings were to be his. He was going to read, he said. All winter long he was either too tired or too busy or too harassed by yammering people to open a book. Now he proposed to get his fill of them and what was more, he declared, he was going to read what he wanted instead of a lot of trash that people forced on him.

There was a big, battered chair in the living room—a comfortable chair in spite of its appearance, which, in Mr. Hobbs' opinion, made it unique among the chairs of Grey Gables. He had appropriated it for his sole use and he would retire to it each evening with a book in his hand. Across the room the Grants and the Carvers would be starting a bridge game and on the other side of the table Mrs. Hobbs was at her never-ending task of knitting baby things. A peaceful hush

fell over the house. The scene reminded Mr. Hobbs of a picture in an old *St. Nicholas* magazine.

The spell was short lived, however, for bridge did not seem to be any deterrent to conversation or argument for either the Carvers or the Grants. As their talk wandered controversially over the entire field of politics, sociology, international relations and the general future of the world, Mr. Hobbs found it more and more difficult to keep his mind on his book.

The Carvers and the Grants seldom seemed to find an area of agreement. To Mr. Hobbs, struggling to prevent himself from being pulled into the current of their talk, it was difficult to know which side he disagreed with most.

He disliked these interminable arguments over questions to which there could be no categorical answer even if the participants had known what they were talking about. He tried to keep out of them. Inevitably, however, some goad sank so deep that he could no longer endure it in silence—and there he was, in the thick of the fight. It was bad for his digestion.

The subjects differed but the pattern remained about the same.

Byron: Did you put on the jack of spades, dear? Well, that's your trick. What I'm trying to say is that all this talk about balanced budgets gives me a pain in the neck. The balanced budget is just as obsolete as the gold standard or the high-wheel bicycle.

Jane: I agree.

("You would," thought Mr. Hobbs, trying to concentrate on his book.)

Susan: You're great ones to talk. You'd balance your budget if you had to starve to do it. Is it my lead?

Jane: Yes, your lead. That's personal. For pity's sake, don't let's get personal.

"I'll tell you all something," said Mr. Hobbs. "If we keep on—"

Byron: I'm not nearly as concerned with balanced budgets as I am with free speech. We're getting into the same state of mind in this country as the Salem witch hunters. Is that your ace?

Stewart: Nobody values free speech more than I do but did it ever occur to your academic mind, Byron, that responsibility goes with freedom. Your trick, dear.

Byron: Words! Same old red herring words. The issue is do we have free speech or don't we! I'll take that.

"I'd like to say something on that point," said Mr. Hobbs.

Peter: (From the second floor) Mommie.

Susan: Free speech doesn't give anyone the right to teach my children treason. Yes, dear, Mommie's here.

"Let me tell you something," said Mr. Hobbs. "If I was a college president I'd fire every goddamn—"

Peter: Mommie, Mommie, Mommie, Mom—

Stewart: For goodness sake, dear, what's the matter with that child?

Susan: Oh he just wants ginger ale. I'll bring him some when we finish this hand.

"I never saw a child consume so much ginger ale in my life," said Mr. Hobbs. "This afternoon—"

Stewart: No one believes in free speech more than I do, but when you're at war—

Jane: That's the kind of a remark I can't stand. It's talk like that that *makes* war.

Susan: I agree with you for once, Jane. What we've got to do in this country is to lead the world into a better way of life by helping those who have less than we have with everything we've got.

Mr. Hobbs put down his book. "Who's going to pay for it?" he shouted.

They stopped playing and looked at him as if he were a stranger who had just emerged through the floor boards.

"*We* are, sir," said Byron. "This *country's* going to pay for it. *We're* going to pay for it out of our boundless resources. It's the price of leadership."

Like an early Christian in a Roman arena Mr. Hobbs looked around for a friendly face. "Where are you going to get the money?" he cried frantically. "Are you going to keep on running this country into debt till the dollar's not worth a plugged nickel or do you want to keep on raising taxes till we're all doing slave labor? Good God, I pay now—"

"The trouble with your generation, sir," said Byron, who had an irritating habit of lowering his voice at such moments, "is that you're using outmoded yardsticks for measuring our economy.—Did you put on the king, Jane?—You keep measuring wealth in terms of dollars and balanced budgets and national debt. Wealth has *nothing* to do with dollars. Dollars are only *symbols*. Wealth is the natural resources of a country—the productivity of its factories—"

"The potential of its labor force," muttered Jane absently. "I seem to be one card shy."

"It's on the floor, dear," said Byron.

Mr. Hobbs ran his finger under the edge of his shirt collar. His voice trembled slightly. "Listen. If dollars don't mean anything then there's something cockeyed about this Island we're living on. It was dollars that bought that beef tonight that you all gobbled up so cheerfully. It was dollars that bought that bottle of gin that disappeared before dinner. Nobody ever handed me any natural resources and I never paid a grocery bill with the potential of a labor force. I wouldn't recognize one if it walked into the room. The trouble with you young fellows is you've got your heads so far in the clouds you can't see the ground. I want to tell you that when I started out—"

"Roger, Roger," said Mrs. Hobbs, continuing to knit placidly. "I don't see why you always get so excited." She held up a half-knitted sweater. "Susan, do you think that's going to be too big for Peter?"

"Looks all right to me, Mother. He'll grow into it if it is."

"Rubber!" shouted Stewart.

"Darling, isn't that Peewee? Will you look, like an angel? She may need changing."

"That was a good rubber," said Jane. "If you'd led your

king of spades the second hand, Susie, I think you'd have
had us on the hook."

"I think I'll go to bed," said Mrs. Hobbs. "The air makes
me sleepy. Coming, Rog?"

"I'm going to take the dogs out for a little while" said Mr.
Hobbs. "I need air."

The two dogs rushed down the front steps and were immediately swallowed up by the darkness. He could hear them
sniffing among the bayberry bushes in their everlasting, eager
hunt for something which was not there.

Crossing the stubby lawn he picked up the path to the
cove. He had no light but the air was luminous from a million stars. It pleased him to discover that some atavistic memory transmitted the feel of the path through his feet and
enabled him to stay on it, if he moved slowly, even though
he could not see it.

He passed the black form of the pumphouse and continued
on down until his feet touched the coarse sand of the cove.
Here the stars seemed to shine with greater brilliance. Far off
to the right the Minamatick Point lighthouse stabbed the
darkness intermittently with its warning beams.

At his feet the small waves broke, pushing up the beach
with a gentle hiss. Mr. Hobbs could hear the occasional sniff
of the dogs as they buried their noses in some particularly
stimulating mess. He suddenly felt less lonely, although up
to that time he had been unaware of any feeling of loneliness. He felt integrated once more, a part of something real.
Filled with content, he felt his way back up the path toward
the house.

15

Mr. Hobbs goes
shopping

Mr. Hobbs had volunteered to do the daily shopping in
Rock Harbor. It was hot and for no obvious reason everyone
seemed a bit out of sorts as people will, periodically, when
they live together in large groups. It struck Mr. Hobbs as a
good morning to be away.

He had planned to make an early start and would have,
had everyone carried out his appointed task. Stewart and
Byron, however, had become involved at breakfast in one of

their interminable discussions. As a result, after many disregarded reminders of the work schedule, Mr. Hobbs himself had as usual disposed of the garbage, started the water pump, thrown away the bottles and burned the paper in addition to doing the living room.

And as usual this ostentatious display of efficiency had hurt Stewart and Byron deeply. Each time he passed them, perched on the rail of the porch, they protested. "Sir, if you'll only *leave* all that we'll do it."

"I can't wait," said Mr. Hobbs grimly.

"But sir, what *difference* does it make if it's not done right away?"

"Because if it's not done right away it's not done at all," snapped Mr. Hobbs.

"But sir, people ought to relax after eating. And besides this is your vacation."

"You're telling *me*," said Mr. Hobbs, sidling through the screen door with five scrap baskets. He allowed it to swing shut with a bang.

"Well, as I was saying," continued Stewart, "I took one look at that valley and I said to my foreman, Benton, 'Listen Joe, you can't do this job with that crew. You'll need at least five hundred men. We'll have to run a narrow gauge from Amityville.' "

There was a brief pause. "I'll never forget how we worked to get that project started. Five weeks, night and day. More than once we worked right around the clock without taking our clothes off. Men worked until they fell asleep exhausted with their heads on their desks. It was good though. It does something to a man's soul to work like that. It opens—"

Mr. Hobbs slammed an empty scrap basket under the living-room table with a metallic clang.

His first stop was at Henry Carter's Gas and Service Station on the edge of the town. The car was seven hundred miles overdue for servicing. It seemed to Mr. Hobbs that it was always seven hundred miles overdue.

The trouble was that it could never be spared long enough to have anything done to it. People were so dependent on their cars these days that they were becoming like centaurs, those strange mythological creatures who were born half man, half horse. Eventually a new race might evolve in which the upper part would be men and women and the lower part automobiles. Mr. Hobbs supposed that when it was time for them to go to the blacksmith shop centaurs had probably had the same difficulty that he did with the car.

When he bought a new car he always read the book of instructions from cover to cover. Then he made out a neatly ruled servicing schedule showing just what should be done each thousand miles for the first thirty servicings. It all seemed so clear and simple as he placed it in the instruction book. Given this kind of loving, systematic care his beautiful new car would last forever.

The first two servicings coincided with the speedometer readings like the teeth of gears. The fact that they were free might have had something to do with it. After that things became confused. When the mileage indicated that it was servicing time either no one noticed it or the car was tied up for days ahead. Sometimes it went to the garage at the end of fifteen hundred miles, sometimes at the end of eighteen hundred, sometimes it skipped a cycle entirely. As a result his schedule became hopelessly confused.

At home, when he was able to pry the car loose, Mr. Hobbs took it to a huge garage, a madhouse of a place which, from the time it opened at eight o'clock until it closed at five, was in a continual state of frenzy. There it would take him half an hour to get anyone to even acknowledge his presence. Eventually after hovering unnoticed around various groups, all engaged in earnest conversation, he would finally succeed in corralling a surly-faced man in a soiled white doctor's coat with "George" embroidered on the pocket.

Now, as everyone knows, this is the point where an automobile owner has a psychic need to tell someone all about his car's special troubles—how at times there is a mysterious tic, tic, tic under the floor boards and how, at other times, the noise goes away—queer, to say the least—how at certain speeds the high-pitched notes of a bird come from the front of the engine—how, when backing up, it sounds as if a gloved hand was rapping against the inside of the luggage compartment.

Such statements are not meant, of course, to insinuate that the car is haunted. They are merely facts that men of motors like to discuss quietly and thoughtfully—and do almost everywhere except in garages like Mr. Hobbs', where the surly-faced man would merely write down his instructions silently on a long form with multiple carbons. Then without so much as an understanding nod he would get into the car, slam the door and start for the opposite wall like a Kamikaze. Just before he crashed he would apply all brakes, causing the hind end to rise as the car stopped in its tracks. Before it settled back on its springs the man in the white coat was out and glowering at another customer.

Men in white coats never knew Mr. Hobbs' name and Mr. Hobbs certainly never had any desire to address them as George. They merely made him wish that he lived in a town where somebody knew who he was. That is why he found Henry Carter such a comfort. The car had scarcely come to a stop before Mr. Carter had his head and shoulders in the front window.

"Well, Mr. Hobbs, how's everything out at Grey Gables?"

"Fine, fine."

"Getting a good rest?"

"Oh swell. Wonderful."

"Good. Store up your strength. You'll need it when you get back to work."

"Thought I'd bring the jalopy in for a little servicing job," said Mr. Hobbs. "Do you want to grease her up and change the oil for me?"

"Sure do," said Mr. Carter. There was a ring in his voice that seemed to say that greasing Mr. Hobbs' car was the kind of a task that any man would undertake with enthusiasm. "Anything else?"

"No, I don't think so," said Mr. Hobbs. "Just grease and oil."

"O.K. Want the filters changed?"

"Well now, I don't know," said Mr. Hobbs uncertainly. "What do *you* think?"

"When'd you have 'em changed last?"

"I can't just remember," said Mr. Hobbs.

"Better change 'em," said Mr. Carter. "How about plugs and points?"

"They *seem* to be all right," said Mr. Hobbs.

"You oughtn't to run 'em more'n ten thousand without changing. Remember when you changed 'em last?"

For the life of him Mr. Hobbs couldn't remember if he'd ever changed them.

Mr. Carter nodded. "Won't do no harm to put in new ones," he said. "Why'n't you let me give the car a thorough going-over? I'll look at everything. Wheels, bearings, transmission, battery, rear end, brakes. The whole works. Then you'll be on the safe side. Saves money in the end."

"It sure does," agreed Mr. Hobbs. "Give it a good going-over. Then I'll know it's been done and I can keep track of things from here in."

"That's right," said Mr. Carter. "I'll put a little sticker on to remind you."

"That's a good idea," said Mr. Hobbs.

As he opened the car door his eye fell on a row of smudged stickers pasted on the door frame—reminders of past reminders. Making sure that Mrs. Hobbs' shopping list was in his pocket he started for Main Street, serene in the knowledge that his interests were in trustworthy hands.

As he passed the Town Hall and Police Headquarters, Chief Peabody walked to a box attached to the corner of the building and, after standing for an instant with his watch in his hand, touched off the noon siren. The impact on his eardrums caused Mr. Hobbs to shy like a horse, then he remembered with dismay that, according to the custom of the Island, all stores were closed from twelve to one.

Store entrances were being locked as he walked slowly down the street trying to decide what to do. The news store on the corner was still open, busily dispensing New York and Boston papers to an eager clientele which was paying a fabulous price to get away from the events about which it now clamored for information.

Mr. Hobbs went in. He might as well pick up some light reading and relax for an hour down by the shore. He looked over the paper-covered books in the racks. They all seemed to be about beautiful young women with loose blouses which were either being torn off by grim-jawed men or were slipping off of their own accord.

Regardless of the titles the pictures were all the same. Mr. Hobbs wondered what would have happened to *Pilgrim's Progress* or *Alice in Wonderland* if they had been born into a world of paper-covered editions. Think what they might have done to *Little Women!*

"Can I help you, sir?" The speaker was a charming young lady in a loose white blouse. Mr. Hobbs felt himself blushing. He seized a book at random, paid for it and hurried out of the store, being careful to keep the front cover concealed against his shirt.

"Good morning, Mr. Hobbs." It was Mrs. Archer Gabrielson looking laundry-fresh in some kind of a loose Tyrolean blouse. "What in the world are you doing all by yourself?"

She noted the book clutched tightly under his arm. "Oh, you like books. I knew it the first time I saw you. What are you reading?"

He felt his color rising again and fought against it desperately. "Oh just trash," he muttered. "How have you been?"

"I adore trash," said Mrs. Archer Gabrielson, reaching for the book. "Let's see."

Mr. Hobbs stepped back in alarm. "I'm afraid I have to hurry along," he said. "They're waiting for me."

"Go and get them," said Mrs. Archer Gabrielson, "and bring them to the house for a cocktail. That's a wonderful idea."

"I wish we could," said Mr. Hobbs, "but the fact is," he glanced about him desperately, "we're due home now. Sickness." Nodding abruptly, he turned and walked rapidly down the street. Mrs. Archer Gabrielson watched him for a moment. She particularly liked eccentric men.

At the end of the street he turned to his left and followed a footpath along the top of the seawall. A narrow strip of beach ran below the wall littered with skiffs, lobster pots, cork floats and the worn gear of professional fishermen. After a while he let himself down onto the beach and found a shady angle between the wall and an old boat. Here he was suddenly cut off from the world—removed as completely from the summer life of Rock Harbor as if he had been on another island.

He wiggled himself into a comfortable position and looked

at the title of the book for the first time. It wall called *Death Lurks in Greenhouses*. How silly! He started to read and as he turned the pages the muscles of his face relaxed. The boat and the seawall faded from his consciousness. Rock Harbor and the Island disappeared and reality was transferred to the characters who moved through the violent world of the printed word.

He looked at his wrist watch incredulously. It was well after two. *Death Lurks in Greenhouses* lay on the sand beside him. He had slumped into the angle between the wall and the boat in a cramped and undignified heap. From the path above he must have resembled one of the numerous corpses in the book. He picked it up from the sand and placed it carefully on one of the seats of the boat. Then he scrambled up the seawall and hurried back to the stores.

Mrs. Hobbs had included swordfish on the list. This involved a trip to Alvin Follensby's Fish Market in Long Beach. Mr. Hobbs picked up the car at Henry Carter's Gas and Service Station. From the length and size of the bill Mr. Carter must have done everything but rebuild it. Such a bill at home would have reduced him to a state bordering on apoplexy. Here he paid it with a smile, shook hands warmly with Mr. Carter and drove away with the comfortable feeling that he had received full value for his money.

Mr. Hobbs liked the drive along the shore to Long Beach. The grass from the salt marshes came down to the sea and the beaches were narrow and shale-covered. On the little bridges across the inlets people fished patiently for crabs with bits of string and fish heads.

The town of Long Beach was built in concentric layers like an onion. One came first to the little bungalows, then the larger cottage-boardinghouses and finally, at the core of the onion, the stores and the long clapboard hotels, trimmed with scrollwork like the perforated paper which Mrs. Hobbs tacked to the edges of her pantry shelves.

On the deep verandahs of these ancient hostelries one might rock comfortably and examine the passers-by on the sidewalk below, or the ceaseless flow of motor cars or even cast an occasional glance at the blue sea beyond and the misty blue sky which rose from its outer edge.

Each bungalow and boardinghouse bore a name displayed

on a painted sign over the porch steps. It was one of the details which distinguished Long Beach from Rock Harbor, where most of the houses passed their years in dignified anonymity. The few that succumbed did so conservatively, calling themselves "The Captain Oliphant Cottage, 1784," or "The Seaview Inn."

In Long Beach, however, there was no such reticence. There self-expression was encouraged and the trend ran to coyness, going to such lengths as "Dew Drop Inn," "Tarryawhile," "Eagle's Nest" and "Harmony Hall."

The Oceanside Hotel dominated all as the monastery dominates a Tibetan village. At this time of day its verandah rail was lined with patrons, rocking mechanically and staring straight ahead with glazed eyes. They were exhausted eyes whose owners, since early morning, had been squeezing every ounce of vacation pleasure from their surroundings.

No small portion of the energies of the new arrivals had been dissipated investigating the attractions advertised by the Oceanside brochure which they had studied so eagerly during the previous winter months. This persuasive mailing piece had indicated by picture and word that the guests of the Oceanside lived in the heart of a sportsman's paradise. Trim sailboats sped through the water at dangerous angles, their lightly dressed crews of bronzed gods and goddesses clinging happily to the windward rails. Laughing beauties, similarly unclad, tore through the water on skis and surfboards. Smartly dressed equestrians galloped along forest trails.

There were photographs of young men on golf tees, exhibiting that amazing follow-through which is only possible when no ball is involved. Young women poised in the pulpits of deep-sea fishing boats, harpoons in readiness for any unwary swordfish that might chance to be strolling by.

And then for those who find this sort of thing tiring on an eight-hour shift, gay groups were shown sitting under striped umbrellas guzzling long drinks and bathers lounged on sandy beaches smiling benignly while the inevitable boy and girl in minimum bathing suits engaged in a non-stop game of leapfrog in the foreground.

For the oldsters there was croquet, played on velvet turf, jovial games of shuffle board and deck tennis where everyone laughed constantly and windswept hills on which to stand and look wistfully toward the horizon. And then, the day's work done, young and old relaxed together by dancing all night to the music of white-coated jazz orchestras.

Of the people who received these brochures and were attracted to Long Beach because of them, not one in a hundred had ever participated in such goings-on or had the slightest desire to do so. They had written too many Department Z-4's, requesting literature, not to know the worst. In spite of that, however, they shared the universal desire of human beings to believe in fairy tales and when reality was forced down their throats they always experienced a brief period of resentment.

The occupants of the rocking chairs on the long porch of the Oceanside had spent a full day, even though it had not been precisely as advertised. They had stood on the boat wharf and watched two boats come in and depart. They had bathed on the narrow beaches, squatting their bodies into the chill water and screaming traditionally. They had thoughtfully twirled a hundred postcard racks and purchased a thick pile of cards which were now lying on their bureaus until they could think up people to whom they might be sent.

Some had bowled, some had ridden on the merry-go-round, a few had even hired rowboats, but the ocean is too big for the cozy feeling which rowing should induce. They had bought saltwater taffy which also lay on their bureaus upstairs. They had bought large clam shells with pictures of the Oceanside hand-painted on their inner surfaces. They had visited the auction sale which went on all day in the store next to the hotel. A few wags had stood by the door, made waggishly low bids and slipped out. An occasional one, blocked by a group just entering, had been stuck with a china vase.

They had gone repeatedly to the mail window in the hotel lobby asking for letters and working themselves up to quite a pitch when there were none. They had walked up and down Ocean Drive in their bathing suits and their new play suits. They had peered at the coral beads in the store windows, drunk an ice cream soda at The-Longest-Soda-Bar-in-the-World, eaten hot buttered popcorn and taken a round of shots in the shooting gallery. Now, exhausted and somewhat toxic, they rocked on the porch of the Oceanside.

Soon they would slip away to their various rooms to scribble on postcards. Then they would sleep until supper. They looked forward to this nap. Later they would go to the enormous frigid movie house opposite the boat dock.

Basically they would have all liked to lie around in complete idleness, letting the hours slip by unnoted. Their time was so short, however, that hours were precious. Out of 365 days there were so few that were truly theirs to dispose of as they wished. This right of disposition became valuable because of its rarity. Failure to exercise it was unthinkable—almost treasonable. To waste time without remorse requires eternity.

Mr. Hobbs had never thought deeply on the subject of swordfish. To him it was just another fish and he regarded all fish as poor man's meat. It was a severe shock to him, therefore, when the youth in rubber boots at Alvin Follensby's Fish Market wrapped his two steaks deftly in brown paper and announced the price as $1.10 a pound.

"My God," said Mr. Hobbs. "I could buy roast beef for less than that."

"Of course," said the young man, obviously appalled by the low level of public intelligence. "This is *sword*fish."

Mr. Hobbs drove home feeling depressed and not a little apprehensive. It was almost five o'clock and he had said he would be home for lunch. Peggy would be tearing her hair out from anxiety.

To his amazement Grey Gables was deserted. He carried the various cartons into the kitchen and placed the swordfish carefully in the icebox, handling it as if it were Steuben glass. Then, feeling abandoned and a bit hurt by the indifference of an empty house, he lay down on the swing couch and was almost immediately asleep.

16

It's a baby's world

Mr. Hobbs' talkative sons-in-law had departed and although eight people were still living within the walls of Grey Gables he had moments of loneliness. Without realizing it he had slipped into a baby's world—a world so fiercely concentrated on the beginnings of life that it had little attention to spare on end products. Stated quite brutally, Mr. Hobbs, who was accustomed to being a motivating force, suddenly found himself cast in the role of a spare tire and it tended to upset his ego.

It was not a world in which he had any real desire to take an active part. He was ill at ease only because he was ignored, even though he knew that it was not premeditated. From what was almost literally dawn to dark Mrs. Hobbs, Susan and Jane spent their time crashing around in the kitchen preparing food for little mouths, trying to push it into them, eventually scraping it into the garbage pail, sloshing water over little bodies, putting them to bed, getting them up, dressing them, undressing them again, hovering over them, rescuing them and picking up after them.

Even in the evening when the last bedroom door had been closed gently for the last time, babies dominated the general conversation. With the odds three to one in favor of their sex, Mrs. Hobbs and her two daughters gave themselves up to the luxury of woman talk. No longer forced, through deference to male interests, to focus their attention on mighty horizons, they let their world shrink to the four walls of Grey Gables and lived contentedly within them.

Occasionally Mr. Hobbs sought to assert himself by venturing a droll story or referring to something that was taking place beyond the confines of the Island. The stories were received with brief and mirthless sounds symbolizing laughter —the kind of amusement sounds that preoccupied people reserve for the very young and the very old and for the anecdotes with which ministers enliven sermons. As for the outside world, Susan and Jane and Mrs. Hobbs had become as oblivious to its existence as a trio of Australian bushwomen.

What depressed him most, however, was that usually when he made these conversational sallies they didn't seem to hear him at all. They were deaf in the same way that a group of adults, interested in their own conversation, do not hear the prattling of a child playing on the floor at their feet.

About the only way that he could be reasonably sure of

commanding attention was to make a sudden and violent noise. The schedule of Quiet Hours, differing as it did for each child, resulted, when consolidated, in an enforced silence for the greater part of each day.

The normal life of Byron Dangerfield Grant, Jr., for example, seemed to call for a more or less perpetual state of coma, as far as Mr. Hobbs could make out. The only time of day during which he appeared officially was from 4 to 5:30 P.M. The remainder of the day he was supposed to be either in a drugged stupor or being fed and both conditions called for silence.

Peewee Carver, on the other hand, gave official voice to her emotions from 6 to 9:30 A.M., a period commonly regarded by normal persons as dedicated to the night's sweetest sleep. By 9:30 she was so exhausted by this premature display of energy that she had to be put to bed for an hour. This was repeated between 1 and 2:30.

Peter was also a lover of the dew-soaked hours, to compensate for which he was thrust forcibly back into bed between 12:30 and 3 in order to recover his strength. As Mr. Hobbs pointed out, if everyone would only co-operate by sleeping a couple of hours longer in the morning they wouldn't conk out in the middle of the day and the rest of the world wouldn't have to wake up in the most sleepable part of the morning.

It was not all as bad as it sounded, however. Once asleep Mr. Hobbs could be quite stubborn about resuming consciousness and there was a blissful period between half past seven and eight each morning when Byron, Jr., had howled himself into a state of exhaustion and Peter and Peewee had stopped banging on the bedroom door and been hauled away to the breakfast table.

A relative silence pervaded Mr. Hobbs' bedroom. He could hear a murmur of voices from the kitchen. Through the open window floated the soothing swoosh of little waves from the Cove. Somewhere over the moors the crows were exclaiming over some repulsive morsel. The drone of a passing plane emerged from nowhere, swelled, and slowly faded out merely emphasizing the silence by its passing. It was an hour for burrowing deeper into the bedclothes and enjoying that delicious half sleep which is one of the true luxuries of a vacation.

There is a flaw in almost every diamond, however. At this moment Mrs. Hobbs was apt to stick her head into the bedroom. "Listen, darling, the girls want to clean up and get off to the beach. It's not fair to them for you to lie here all day. After all it's their vacation, you know."

Experience had taught him that it was useless to argue this point. He would kill a few more minutes after Mrs. Hobbs had left staring at the ceiling and trying to figure out *why* the girls couldn't clean up and get off to the beach even if he should lie in bed for the rest of the month. This inevitably led to the conclusion that, if he stayed in bed *all* the time, he wouldn't be holding up anything. It was only because he got up regularly that he couldn't lie in bed as long as he wanted. It was too complicated for early morning rumination. He preferred getting up.

The beach referred to was not the Pirates' Cove, but a huge crescent of ivory-colored sand between Grey Gables and Rock Harbor. The land which lay behind its dunes was boggy, or in some other way unsuitable for human exploitation, and because of this lucky circumstance the setting of the beach was unmarred by improvements except for a sandy track which led to it from the main road.

No cabanas or bathhouses interrupted the symmetrical curves of the dunes. No summer cottages broke the skyline behind them. Even the automobiles of the bathers were forced by the loose sand to remain out of sight. Here the good folk of Rock Harbor were apt to gather for some part of each day— longer or shorter depending on whether they were still at the age when the texture of their skin was so perfect that they could be careless about it.

About eleven o'clock the first striped umbrella blossomed suddenly on the glaring sands. An hour later they bloomed like a brilliant garden from one horn of the crescent to the other. The lazy and the gregarious clustered near the entrance opening. The isolationists, the individualists, the gymnasts and the big groups moved out on either side.

There being no bathhouses, people arrived in bathing suits except for a few who dressed in the doubtful privacy of the dunes. As each group filed through the gap onto the beach it resembled a nomadic desert tribe moving to new pastures. Each tribesman bore his burden, from the tiniest tot, staggering drunkenly through the dry sand, to the elders protected like alpine climbers from the sun's glare, and laden with equipment.

Primitive man undoubtedly walked unencumbered to the nearest beach, dunked his body and went home—if he bathed at all, which is doubtful. The National Association of Manufacturers has done away with this intolerable situation, however, and seen to it that no good American goes anywhere empty-handed—particularly to beaches. In consequence these modern nomads bore colorful loads made up of folded umbrellas, striped back rests, rubber rings, cameras, inflated rubber horses, Scotch plaid food pails, thermos cases, sunburn lotion, surfboards, rubber rafts, pails and shovels, swimming feet, striped sand towels, and, of course, portable radios.

One could tell the Newcomers from the Old-timers at a glance. The former were apt to appear merely carrying bath towels. They sat huddled in little groups, caught between the fierce light of the sun and the reflected rays of the sea and sand, gazing miserably and shamefacedly at the luxury surrounding them. They took to the water soon in self-protection and shortly after retreated to their cars under the scornful eyes of the Old-timers reclining in their encampments.

To watch a group of Old-timers pick a site and go into action was reminiscent of the golden days of the road circus. The leader would select a spot where the sand was not too hot and dry or too damp and cold and which was out of reach of the incoming tide. One squint at the sun and the umbrella was up at just the right angle to give maximum shadow. Almost at the same instant the picnic gear was stowed, the elders, black-goggled and shiny, seated in the shade casting preliminary looks of disapproval at their neighbors, the male youth rushing into the sea with high-raised knees, hurling their surfboards over the tops of the waves, the glistening female youth, goggled and shut-eyed, stretched in a row on beach towels in the full glare of the sun, a radio at their heads like a super-modern tombstone, children dashing to the water's edge then retreating with shrill screams, infants staggering and collapsing in the loose sand by the dunes and dogs, dazed by their sudden freedom, running about in circles and barking out of sheer delight.

On week days the Summer Widows were apt to arrive about eleven-thirty—a huge group dragging their offspring behind them. They had their special, undisputed dune, well down the beach, in the meager shade of which they camped daily.

They were an attractive, brown-skinned lot, the Summer Widows, as they lay about in a great circle, each surrounded by her own belongings, through and over which her brood crawled and stumbled.

Looking them over Mr. Hobbs could not decide whether to rejoice in the beauty of their young maternity or deplore such a waste of good-looking girls. Beautiful women without men did not harmonize with summer beaches.

Viewed under the remorseless glare of a noonday sun, it struck him that modern women led rather a squaw's life. He felt distinctly sorry for them, particularly the Young Mothers. Like Gelett Burgess and his purple cow, he decided that he would rather see than be one.

Women took so long to get going. They could not seem to think ahead. Mr. Hobbs, for example, got up, had his breakfast, did the chores and then was ready for the beach. For him it was as simple as that. To Susan, Jane and Mrs. Hobbs, however, starting for the beach seemed to involve almost insuperable problems.

First, of course, there was the question of who was going to stay behind with Byron, Jr., and, usually, Peewee. The resulting arguments vacillated between two extremes. They had a barometric quality. Either everyone insisted on being a martyr (which meant the day was either chilly or over-cast) or everyone regarded themselves as having been im-posed on long enough (which meant fair weather). What annoyed Mr. Hobbs was that no one ever gave the matter a thought until he backed the car out of the garage and sat, with the engine running, waiting for them to get in.

Next came the assembling of the gear, another haphazard performance by Mr. Hobbs' standards. Gradually, however, after an interminable wait and much tooting of the horn, the back of Susan's station wagon was piled with beach-battered miscellany and everyone was in place.

"Rog, don't go a minute! My dark glasses! Oh dear, did anybody see my dark glasses?"

"Mother, they're just where you left them. On the kitchen table."

"Rog, dear, will you just dash in and have a look, like an angel. I'm no good on that beach without those dark glasses."

And then, as the screen door slammed behind him, "Pops, I'm sorry, I forgot my bath towel. It's the pink one behind the bathroom door. And while you're in the house will you see if you can find my book?"

"There," said Mrs. Hobbs complacently as Mr. Hobbs slid

behind the wheel once more. "Now *think*, Rog, whether you've forgotten anything else. There's no use getting down there and having to come all the way back."

The parking space behind the dunes was a dangerous area where cars were apt to back suddenly into the unwary bather as he dreamily flicked the wet sand off his feet and ran the edges of his damp bath towel between his toes. It was a place where child-crazed mothers were constantly maneuvering their cars into soft spots in the sand beside the track, causing rear wheels to dig deeper and deeper and rear ends to chatter and shake until soft-hearted bathers pushed them out.

"Now, children, don't run off and let Bompa carry everything," said Mrs. Hobbs. "Here, Peter, you take your ring and your towel. You take the radio and the thermos case, Susan, and I'll take this stuff."

Selecting their burdens they would trudge off happily, leaving Mr. Hobbs to cope with what was left. This usually consisted of all the unmanageable articles, the beach umbrella whose sharp-ended pole was always slipping off his shoulder and threatening to pierce his foot like a javelin, the picnic basket and the back rests which he could only carry by pressing them painfully against his body with his elbow. He comforted himself with the thought that no one had as yet invented a portable beach television set.

It was all worth it though as he lay in the buoyant water, floating on his back with arms outstretched. The waves, hurrying shoreward, passed beneath him in a succession of soft bumps. He watched the terns circling over the water a few yards out, their heads bent downward in fierce concentration. Occasionally one dropped, like a stone, and then seemed to bounce upward from the surface of the sea, a silver glint protruding from its beak.

From the beach behind him came the sound of children's voices, the occasional bark of a dog and the rhythmic, velvet crunch of the small waves.

Here, in this brief moment, he found the fulfillment of all his vague winter dreams. This was the moment that he would carry away with him in his memory—an experience so vivid, so richly-colored that it would be as clear to him months hence as something seen through a window.

"Where's Kate?" asked Mr. Hobbs.

Mrs. Hobbs looked at him with unbelieving eyes. "What do you mean 'Where's Kate?'"

"I mean 'Where's Kate?'" said Mr. Hobbs irritably.

"Why, darling, you know perfectly well she's visiting that Cranford girl at Harwichport. I *do* wish you'd try to collect yourself and pay attention. It isn't attractive to be so vague."

"I *do* pay attention. Nobody ever tells me anything. What Cranford girl?"

"*Jane* Cranford. Kate's friend from Detroit."

"I never heard of her."

"Why Roger Hobbs! She visited us last Christmas vacation. I think you're getting senile."

Mr. Hobbs grunted and returned to his book. Kate confused him although he wouldn't have admitted it. No child of his had ever succeeded in living such a complex life. As a result he seemed to have lost touch with her completely during the last few years. Once he had thought that they were unusually close to one another. Then she had suddenly gone underground like those queer rivers that disappear without warning into desert sands. He had hoped to pick up the ties again during these weeks at Grey Gables, but the child was never there and nobody even bothered to tell him where she was.

Now that Mr. Hobbs thought about it, Kate had been acting queerly for some time. For instance she had always eaten like a horse in defiance of a figure that was never meant for that sort of thing. She had always preferred blue jeans to dresses and her normal contempt for all things masculine was withering. Then suddenly she had ceased eating almost completely—she never passed a mirror without stopping in front of it—she spent hours in her room pulling her hair this way and that and the hitherto despised males were in her life from morning till night.

Too many automobiles, that was what was the matter. All these young pretty boys seemed to own automobiles as soon as they got out of their baby carriages. They'd be putting motors on kiddie cars next. It went to girls' heads. Like that silly ass in the convertible with all the gadgets that came for Kate the other night. How did *he* rate a car? As a matter of fact, now that he thought of it, he'd seen that red convertible drive in more than once. Silly ass with a crew cut.

"How did she get up to Harwichport?" he asked.

"I told you yesterday, dear. She drove up with the Griswold boy."

"The who boy?"

"Darling, Sam Griswold. The one that comes to see Kate all the time in the red convertible."

Mr. Hobbs straightened up in his chair. "Don't tell me you let her go off with that specimen?"

"Listen, Rog. In the first place Sam Griswold is not a specimen. He's a *very nice boy*. In the second place Kate is a sophomore in Smith this fall. She doesn't need a nursemaid any more."

"Maybe so. I'm not sure she doesn't need a psychiatrist though. Have you noticed that child lately, Peggy? When she's home, which isn't often, God knows, she picks at her food like a bird and she never opens her mouth. Spends most of her time in her room in front of her mirror. I opened her door the other night and she was standing in front of it making faces. I tell you, Peggy, that child has been going too hard. She's exhausted."

Mrs. Hobbs knitted for some time in silence. "Did it ever occur to you, Rog, that Kate might be in love?"

Mr. Hobbs put down his book. "Kate?" he exclaimed incredulously. "Kate? Who'd be in love with Kate?"

"Well, Sam Griswold, for instance."

"That irresponsible ass!" shouted Mr. Hobbs. "That hot rod plumber! That's what happens when you let your children go running all over the country with every Tom, Dick and Harry."

"How do you know he's an ass, dear? Now look, Rog, you've been all through this twice before. Why don't you save yourself the wear and tear and get used to the fact that the last of your children has grown up."

17

House guests

Mr. Hobbs awoke with an uneasy feeling that there was something wrong. For a moment he couldn't recollect what it was. Then he remembered. Guests were arriving. The thought was so distasteful to him that he pulled the bed-clothes over his head and tried to recapture sleep. Mrs. Hobbs was moving about the room.

"Please get up, Rog. I don't know how I'm ever going to get this place ready as it is."

Mr. Hobbs took advantage of the opening. "What in the world is there to do?" he asked. "You always fuss so. We pick up the Turners on the three o'clock boat. Some people come for cocktails at half past five. They drink them, they go home and that's that. The thing that gets me though is why you asked the Turners in the first place."

"Why *I* asked them! *You* were the one that insisted on their coming. Now please don't just lie there being difficult. You *promised* me that you'd weed the terrace before the cocktail party and you haven't done it. You promised to fix the screen door latch so it doesn't fall apart every time the door slams. It isn't done. There's a mountain of cartons to be burned. I don't believe you've—"

"O.K., O.K.," said Mr. Hobbs. "I just don't like to be hurried so, that's all." He threw his bathrobe over his shoulders and shuffled off in the direction of the Cove.

The sun was still close to the horizon as he descended the path to the beach. The water in the little cove was like a silver mirror. Beyond the point, where it joined the open sea, it turned suddenly blue as an off-shore breeze darkened its surface like rubbed velvet. On an exposed rock a few yards off the point a gull brooded. As Mr. Hobbs waded into the water it flapped away, complaining loudly. A family of tiny crabs scuttled from beneath his feet, escaping death by inches.

It was a part of the day which seemed to belong particularly to the Island and to all the living creatures which lived on it and above it and in the waters around it—all, that is, except Mr. Hobbs. He felt like an interloper—an awkward guest who arrives before the appointed hour.

He plunged in with a splash and, burying his face beneath the surface, thrashed violently through the water for several feet, using what he conceived to be a crawl stroke. Having made this concession to virility he turned over on his back and paddled slowly out to the gull's rock, watching the strands of mist along the shore vanish slowly before the onslaught of the morning sun.

What in the world was he going to do with Martin Turner and his wife for two days? He hardly knew them. At the moment he couldn't even remember clearly what they looked

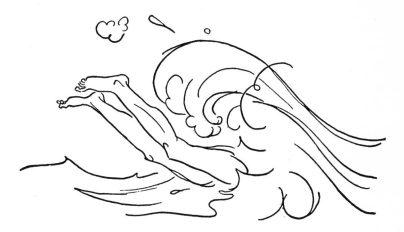

like, but five months ago, sitting in the sun-drenched court-yard of an Arizona ranch, he had regarded them as intimate friends. When they had announced that they were motoring up the New England coast during August the most natural thing in the world was to ask them to spend a couple of nights on the Island. Now, as he thought of all the real friends they should have invited to visit Grey Gables and hadn't, the whole thing became completely inexplicable to him.

He dried himself thoughtfully, climbed the path and examined the half circle of lawn at the top, bordered by beds of sun-baked zinnias, which Mrs. Hobbs referred to as the terrace and which he had promised to weed. It was hard to tell which were weeds and which crab grass.

He looked over the cartons and the empty bottles outside the kitchen door and then went on to the clothes yard to hang up his towel.

The deep-throated greeting of the *Island Queen* shattered the calm of the summer afternoon as the white car-ferry rounded the buoy and headed for the dock. Mr. and Mrs. Hobbs stood beside a weather-beaten pile and watched its approach with somber faces.

As the *Queen* drew near the dock, however, Mrs. Hobbs, who was always quick at such things, recognized their guests on the upper deck and her expression immediately changed to one of eager animation. "There's Emily," she cried, plucking at Mr. Hobbs' sleeve. "See. In the floppy red hat. Imagine wearing a hat like that on a boat. That's Martin right behind her. Yoo-hoo, Emily."

Mr. Hobbs disliked being plucked. "I see, I see," he said crossly, without relaxing his smile. "Don't go all to pieces." He clasped his hands and shook them over his head like a fighter entering a ring.

The ferry crashed against the piles. The Martin Turners disappeared into the crowd that was fighting its way slowly down the narrow metal stairs to the main deck. Animation faded from the faces of Mr. and Mrs. Hobbs like sunlight shut off by a passing cloud.

Five minutes later the sun shone once more, however. "There they are," cried Mrs. Hobbs. "There's Emily just in front of the milk truck. They must have left their car on the Mainland. I guess they put it in a garage to save the cost of bringing it over."

"Garage my eye," said Mr. Hobbs. "I'll bet they left it on the street and saved some more money."

The Turners staggered up the ramp, their knees buckling under the weight of suitcases. Mrs. Hobbs rushed toward them with outstretched arms. "Emily!" she cried. "Emily! How perfectly wonderful!"

"Peggy!" cried Mrs. Turner, dropping her suitcases in the middle of the ramp. "This is *too* exciting!"

They embraced, each kissing the air beside the other's right ear. Mr. Turner dropped his suitcases also. The disembarking passengers flowed around them like a stream around a rock. A few, failing to notice them, stumbled over them and glared balefully.

Mr. Hobbs and Mr. Turner seized hands and pumped vigorously. "Well, well, Martin," said Mr. Hobbs heartily. "Welcome aboard."

"Glad to see you, Hobbs," said Mr. Turner, "and we're certainly glad to get here after *that* trip. Zowie, what a tub!"

Mr. Hobbs hated being called Hobbs. It made him feel like a stage butler. He also resented strangers making disparaging remarks about the *Island Queen,* but this was no time to register annoyance. "Here, let me take your things," he said. "We had to park our car about two blocks away."

He bent his knees slightly to pick up the two enormous suitcases which Mr. Turner had been carrying. At the first tug he glanced down to see if they were caught on anything.

"I don't know why you should do that, old man," said Mr. Turner, making no attempt to prevent him. "But if you're going to insist I'll take Emily's."

"Damn decent not to make me come back for them," muttered Mr. Hobbs, but he knew they could not hear him as the three of them had already started walking up the dock, laughing and chattering.

Mr. Hobbs trundled after them slowly with the great bags. They stuck out like tanks on either side, making it impossible for him to move through the crowd without knocking them against people's legs.

When he arrived at the car, Mrs. Hobbs was alone. "Martin and Emily have gone to look for some kind of a light filter for their camera," she said. "They've gone in for three-dimensional color pictures. They're so interesting. They always have something new. Their daughter has just been married. You remember her—very tall and pretty. She married that boy—" But Mr. Hobbs did not hear her. He was trying to force the huge suitcases into the baggage compartment without getting a hernia.

Half an hour later the Turners reappeared. They had not only found just the filter they were looking for but had also discovered an enchanting book called *Our Island Birds.*

"You probably have it at the house," said Mr. Turner. "But it's something we wanted anyway."

Mr. Hobbs couldn't make out whether they were giving it to him or not so he merely said he didn't think he had it.

"Let's show off the Island!" cried Mrs. Hobbs gaily. "We'll take Emily and Martin home by the Headland Road. It will be beautiful today."

Anything that promised to kill time until the cocktail party was agreeable to Mr. Hobbs. They wound their way through the traffic of Long Beach, talking eagerly about mutual friends at the ranch. Mr. Hobbs had a sickening feeling that, once they reached the end of the list, conversation would be about over.

Eventually the road emerged from a forest of scrub pine onto the broad moorlands. It wound across their gentle folds, climbing steadily until it reached the edge of the cliffs. Far below the ocean rolled in to a broad beach, its noiseless waves breaking and moving shoreward in thin, parallel lines of white. Beyond, the deep blue waters of the Atlantic glittered in the late afternoon sun.

Mr. Turner was sitting in front with Mr. Hobbs. "I suppose you do a lot of photography in a place like this," he said.

"Peggy's the photographer in our family," said Mr. Hobbs. "She takes a new picture of the kids every five minutes."

"What does she use?" asked Mr. Turner.

"A camera," said Mr. Hobbs, surprised.

"Did you ever try a Strobex for that kind of work?" said Mr. Turner. "If you ever used a Strobex with a super-speed lens I'll bet you'd never put up with anything else."

Mr. Hobbs, who didn't know what Mr. Turner was talking about, said he'd have to try one sometime.

"It gives you depth," said Mr. Turner. "I never got such depth with any other combination. You ought to send for one."

"How do you like our view?" interrupted Mrs. Hobbs.

Mr. Turner glanced toward the ocean. "The only trouble

with a view like that," he said, cocking his head slightly and squinting one eye, "is that it has no center of interest. I hear you do a lot of portrait work."

"Who, me?" There was dismay in Mrs. Hobbs' voice.

"You ought to get Rog to give you one of those new Strobexes," advised Mr. Turner. "I was just selling him the idea. If you're trying to get depth there's the camera for you. In a light like this at f8—" He was still talking when they drew up before Grey Gables.

Mr. Hobbs gave an involuntary grunt as he pulled one of the big suitcases from the baggage compartment. "Aren't those awful?" said Mrs. Turner. "When you come to a place like this, though, you never can tell what you are in for, so Martin and I just bring everything. Why don't you let Martin take them, Rog? He has a bad back, but if he tackles them one at a time and rests on the way they probably won't do him any harm."

"I wouldn't think of it," gasped Mr. Hobbs.

"At least I can hold the door open for you, old man," said Mr. Turner, bounding past him up the front steps.

Mr. and Mrs. Turner, Mr. and Mrs. Hobbs, Jane, Susan and Peter were assembled on the grass terrace which Mr. Hobbs had weeded so laboriously only a few hours before. It seemed to him that it looked rather ratty without the weeds, but once it was covered with people no one would notice it.

The Turners were dressed to the nines. Mr. Turner wore an immaculate white coat, rusty red trousers and blue canvas shoes with thick crepe rubber soles. Mrs. Turner had on some kind of an embroidered peasant's costume and was weighted down with colored necklaces and bracelets. She gave Mr. Hobbs the feeling that she might break out into grand opera at any minute. Mr. Hobbs, in a pair of old gray flannels, felt like a tramp.

He was too tired to care much, however. While the Turners had been resting, he had been staggering back and forth between the house and the terrace carrying tables, chairs, ice buckets, glasses, bottles and platters of stuffed eggs and spreads. Now he relaxed wearily in a canvas chair.

"We might have a quick one before the others get here," he suggested.

"Martin and I don't drink," said Mrs. Turner.

"You don't *drink?*" said Mr. Hobbs. It was a cry, not a question.

"Haven't touched the stuff since we saw you at the ranch," said Mr. Turner. "Emily didn't care for it—never has—and what she doesn't care for I don't and vice versa."

"You *see*, Rog," said Mrs. Hobbs reproachfully.

Mr. Hobbs immediately asserted himself by mixing a short highball. "I suppose you two are bridge fiends," he said, in an exploratory way. He might as well find out the worst and have it over with.

"We don't play cards," said Mrs. Turner. "They bore Martin almost to death."

"I don't suppose you want to do anything after the party tonight anyway," said Mrs. Hobbs. "You must be tired after your trip. Rog is planning to run you over to the Country Club in the morning. I notice you didn't bring any clubs, but he can fit you out."

"Martin doesn't play golf," said Mrs. Turner. "He used to,

but he gave it up. We can't *stand* married couples who split up every weekend over golf. Don't you feel that way?"

Mr. Hobbs dodged the question. "Perhaps you both play tennis," he said. "Peggy and I are too ancient, but Susan and Jane will give you a good workout."

"No thanks, old man," said Mr. Turner. "We don't play tennis either. As a matter of fact we don't go in for any of those Country Club activities. Emily and I lead a very simple life. In the winter we like to chum around together at concerts and galleries and that sort of thing. And when the good old summertime comes along we just like to get out in the open with our camera and a pair of fieldglasses. We adored the ranch, as you know, and our desert rides together, but the best thing of all is to get out on your own trotters and see what you can see. By the way, Hobbs, are you a bird spotter?"

Mr. Hobbs was so sunk by the impact of what he had heard in the last few minutes that he jumped, like one who has been unexpectedly goosed. "I'm *interested* in birds," he said, somewhat amazed at his own words.

Mrs. Hobbs shared his amazement. "Why, Roger Hobbs— you don't know a crow from a cuckoo."

"We keep a season score," said Mr. Turner, ignoring her. "Two hundred and forty-four so far this year. Not bad for August."

"Two hundred and forty-four what?" asked Mr. Hobbs.

Mr. Turner looked at him suspiciously. "Species," he said. "Different kinds of birds. We'll take you out tomorrow morning. Got any glasses?"

Mr. Hobbs said he had.

"What power and field?" asked Mr. Turner.

"I don't know," said Mr. Hobbs.

"Well, you can use ours," said Mr. Turner, the implication being that a man like Mr. Hobbs was sure to have the wrong kind anyway.

A car turned in the driveway. "Oh thank God," said Mrs. Hobbs, who during the last ten minutes had reached the sickening conclusion that none of her outside guests were going to show.

Once they started to come they arrived so rapidly that Mr. Hobbs became completely occupied mixing drinks. He was no longer one of the party and nobody pretended that he was. After they had received a wet handshake from him they went about *their* business and left him to *his*.

Apparently everyone that Mrs. Hobbs had asked also had guests of their own—guests whom they were only too glad to jettison temporarily into someone else's party. They sat about on the canvas chairs and the prickly grass talking in the easy manner of people who have known one another all their lives. Mr. Hobbs remembered the names of a few, a number of faces had a familiar look to him—the majority, however, he could not recollect ever having seen before.

He passed among them, watching for empties, like an efficient *maître d'hôtel*. Some nodded pleasantly and even murmured a few words while handing him their glasses as, in the days of servants, one might have said a few words to an old family retainer while handing him one's hat and stick. Most of them, however, allowed him to remove the glasses

from their inert fingers without interrupting their conversations.

When he asked what kind of a refill was expected they looked at him with the irritated eyes of those who have been clumsily disturbed. Then their faces would light with momentary recognition. "Oh, thanks, Mr. Hobbs. That was a little Scotch on the rocks with just a dash of water," or "I had a bourbon with half a teaspoonful of sugar and a twist of peel—but *no bitters*." This admonition was always given in a severe, threatening tone indicating that if there was any further sloppiness something would be done about the matter.

Mr. Hobbs struggled to remember the various combinations. He was sure that he made many mistakes, but no one seemed to notice them so he relaxed. He was also conscientious at first about giving the right glass back to its original user. As the pressure mounted, however, he lost all feeling for these niceties and merely kept a paper napkin in his pocket with which to remove lipstick from the edge of a refill before handing it to a male customer.

Peter had been groomed within an inch of his life for the role of hors d'oeuvre passer and Mrs. Hobbs glowed with grandmatronly pride as her female guests paid tribute. "My dear, he looks like a little angel." "The cutest thing I ever saw."

For some reason the world assumes that young children are incapable of understanding the simplest statements of their elders. It is an error of judgment that frequently produces unfortunate results.

In this case the subject of the eulogies was not nearly as

pleased by them as were his mother and grandmother. As he passed the platters of stuffed eggs and sticky spreads, he directed a glare of hatred at each admirer and continued to stare angrily over his shoulder as he moved away until, eventually, the contents of the plate slid onto the grass and over the shoes of the guests.

Because Peter was not their child this was considered cute. He was soon relieved, but it was too late. The damage had been done. Deprived of his props and noting the consequent decline in his attention value, he switched to a new act. Extending his arms he began to execute a kind of one-man ballet among the guests.

Mrs. Hobbs and Susan pretended not to notice, but as person after person began to mop themselves with paper napkins, Mrs. Hobbs was forced into the action which she had dreaded.

"Peter, dear, it's time for bed and *do* watch what you're doing. (I'm *so* sorry. Please let Rog get you another.) *Stop* it, Peter. (Oh dear, I do hope it doesn't stain. That's such a heavenly blue.) Come now, Peter. That's enough. We're going to bed."

Peter backed behind a chair. "No," he said.

"Susan, will you *please*— Come now, darling. No nonsense."

"I don't like you," said Peter. "Or you. Or you. Or you—" Susan's hand closed over his wrist and he disappeared suddenly from the midst of the group. A number of guests turned startled faces as his scream of protest split the summer air.

Mr. Hobbs stopped sloshing about at his card table bar.

"Good God," he said, "what's the matter with that child anyway?"

"He's tired, poor lamb," said Mrs. Hobbs.

"Do you suppose I could have a tiny dash of bourbon?" said a strange man with a huge mustache.

It was nine o'clock when the last noisy carload of guests disappeared into the night. Apparently the Islanders' ideas about dining were vague, if they had any at all. The Turners had been fed eventually on scraps. Susan and Jane had taken over in the kitchen. In the living room Mrs. Hobbs and Mrs. Turner had begun on the ranch people all over again. This time they were doing a thorough job which could last indefinitely. Mr. Hobbs was running a shuttle service between the house and the littered terrace, retrieving debris.

Mr. Turner accompanied him on these sorties like an escort fighter plane, occasionally carrying a couple of glasses or a cigarette box, but mostly just talking.

"The older I get," he was saying, "the more convinced I am that the outdoors furnishes a man with every pleasure that he can possibly wish for—and free at that. Do you ever read Thoreau any more?"

Mr. Hobbs admitted that he had fallen out of the habit.

"That's not right," cried Mr. Turner. "Everybody should have Thoreau on his bed table. I'll send you a copy of *Walden* when we get back. Remind me to put that down. It comes in a cheap edition. You'll love reading it again. No man since Thoreau—"

"Do you mind holding the screen door open for me?" inter-

rupted Mr. Hobbs. He sidled through the doorway, sandwiched between two bridge tables.

Mrs. Turner called cheerily from the living room. "Why don't you two boys relax? You'll both be worn out. Tomorrow is another day, you know."

"I think you're absolutely right," said Mr. Turner. "And what's more, if you folks don't mind, Emily and I are going to turn in. I don't know how you feel, but we think the best part of the day is the early morning—just after sunrise. That's when everything is fresh and sparkling. Do you remember how Emily and I used to go for a before-breakfast walk every morning at the ranch?"

At the ranch Mr. Hobbs had always slept until the final breakfast bell, so he didn't remember.

"How about *you,* old man? Aren't you going to turn in and enjoy this wonderful sea air?"

"Not till I clean up this goddamn mess," said Mr. Hobbs somewhat rudely.

"Well I hate to desert you, but you don't mind if we call it a day, do you?"

"Not a bit," said Mr. Hobbs.

18

The bird spotters

"Look!" cried Mr. Hobbs excitedly. "There's a big bunch—over there—sitting on the telephone wire."

"Barn swallows," said Mr. Turner, scarcely glancing at them.

"I don't see how you can tell," said Mr. Hobbs admiringly. To him they were just so many gray-black beads strung on the wire.

"Couldn't be anything else," said Mr. Turner, "the way they're bunched and everything. Then look at the marking. That cinnamon buff underneath and the white spots on the tail. Barn swallows are the only ones with white spots on their tails."

"That's very interesting," said Mr. Hobbs. He borrowed Mr. Turner's fieldglasses and studied the barn swallows carefully. He could see no cinnamon buff undersides and if there were any white spots on their tails they were sitting on them. To him they were still gray-black balls strung on a telephone wire.

"See what I mean?" asked Mr. Turner.

"Absolutely," said Mr. Hobbs.

Mr. Turner looked pleased. "You're going to be a good bird spotter," he said.

Immediately after breakfast Mr. Turner had insisted on taking Mr. Hobbs for a bird walk. Mrs. Turner had volunteered to stay home and keep Mrs. Hobbs company.

"This time of year we ought to identify about thirty-five," said Mr. Turner at breakfast.

"Thirty-five is a teeny bit high," contradicted Mrs. Turner sweetly. "Some have migrated. Thirty-three might be nearer."

"Thirty-three to thirty-five," said Mr. Turner. "I like to give myself lots of leeway." They both laughed heartily as if this was an excellent joke.

The barn swallows had been their first identification. Mr. Turner took a pad and pencil out of his pocket. "Here," he said. "You keep score." Mr. Hobbs wrote "Barn Swallows."

Mr. Turner walked with a long springy stride. Mr. Hobbs found it difficult to keep up with him. Mr. Turner glanced at him from time to time. "You've never done much walking, have you?" he said.

"What do you mean?" said Mr. Hobbs. "I've been walking

ever since I was a baby." He was getting tired of this sort of thing.

"You don't walk right," said Mr. Turner. "You wouldn't last any time at all walking like that. You walk with your knees stiff. You ought to bend them at each step. Exaggerate it a bit and you'll get the idea. Walk as if you were sitting down." Half squatting they walked painfully down the road for several minutes. An automobile came up unexpectedly from behind them. The occupants of the back seat turned to stare at them from the rear window.

"Get the idea?" said Mr. Turner.

"Yes indeed," said Mr. Hobbs, straightening his legs with relief.

"You come down too hard on your *heels*," said Mr. Turner severely. "Try to have the whole foot touch the ground at the same instant—*and don't toe out* like a duck. Try toeing in for a while. That will break you of the habit."

Mr. Hobbs tried it although he hated himself for doing so. He felt as if he was about to dislocate every joint from his knees down. What did this maniac think he was? An India rubber man? When he thought Mr. Turner's attention was diverted he resumed his normal way of walking.

"There we are," said Mr. Turner, so suddenly that Mr. Hobbs started. "Put down a chickadee."

"Where?" asked Mr. Hobbs. His voice was tense and he darted glances in all directions as if he expected to see a cloud of maddened chickadees come charging down on them from a tree top.

"Over there somewhere," said Mr. Turner, waving his hand

toward a clump of trees. "Can't you *hear* it? It goes chick-a-dee-dee-dee." Mr. Turner made thin squeaking noises. Mr. Hobbs listened intently. All he could hear were some crickets in an adjoining field.

"Oh yes," he said, and wrote "chickadee" on the pad under "barn swallow." He began to feel like the Helen Keller of the bird world.

They walked in silence for a few minutes. "Those aren't very good shoes for this sort of thing," said Mr. Turner.

"I know they're not much to look at," said Mr. Hobbs, "but they're awfully comfortable."

"You need something that will hug the foot more. The Austrians make the best walking shoe. These were made for me in Austria. I advise you to get a pair if you're going to do this sort of thing much. But it doesn't matter this morning because we're not going to get very far." His tone indicated that if the expedition had not been shackled to a ball and chain like Mr. Hobbs it might have accomplished something. "There's a flight of chewink."

Mr. Hobbs looked among the trees beside the road, but could see nothing.

"You're looking in the wrong place," said Mr. Turner impatiently. "Over on the skyline above those woods."

Squinting, Mr. Hobbs was able to distinguish some tiny dots above the distant trees. They could also have been gnats flying around his face.

"I don't see how you can be *completely* sure they're chewink," he said.

"Line of flight," said Mr. Turner. "Chewinks fly this way."

He illustrated with the palm of his hand. "Can't miss 'em. Well that's *three* species you know. Now *you* try identifying them. That's the way to learn."

Mr. Hobbs wrote down "chewink" and proceeded down the road, staring so hard into the trees and bushes that his eyeballs felt as if they were protruding. "Not many birds out this afternoon," he said conversationally.

"Oh yes there are," said Mr. Turner. "There are hundreds of 'em in those bushes and trees. They've all been barn swallows or chewinks. I thought you—"

"There's one!" cried Mr. Hobbs. He wanted so much to spot it before Mr. Turner that his voice was almost a scream. "What was it?"

"Barn swallow," said Mr. Turner. "You won't see much of anything else around here. I want to work down through that patch of woods to the left. We might stir up something and there should be birds in those fields down near the shore."

A wagon track led off the road and across the fields to the woods which Mr. Turner had indicated. The entrance was barred by a gate. Mr. Turner started to climb between the rails. "There's a sharp-shinned hawk," he cried suddenly. At the moment his head was between the rails and Mr. Hobbs looked instinctively at the ground around his feet. Mr. Turner, still half suspended in the gate pointed upward and to the left. Mr. Hobbs saw a small bird disappearing behind a tree in the field ahead.

"Why are their shins sharper than other hawks?" he asked.

"They're not," said Mr. Turner. "They have a square-tipped tail. You can tell them by that."

"I see," said Mr. Hobbs. He wrote "sharp-tipped hawk" on the pad. He didn't write very legibly as Mr. Turner never slowed down and he found it difficult to write while hurrying down a rough wagon track.

Mr. Turner froze suddenly and whipped his fieldglasses out of their case. He studied a clump of trees to the right, then handed the glasses to Mr. Hobbs. "Want to see a red-eyed vireo?" he asked in a low voice.

"Yes," whispered Mr. Hobbs. His hands trembled slightly as he took the glasses. He examined the clump of trees from their roots to their topmost branches. All he could see was a slight movement of leaves caused by the soft August breeze. "I'll be damned," he said, handing the glasses back to Mr. Turner.

"Ever see one before?" asked Mr. Turner.

"Never," said Mr. Hobbs.

"First one I've seen this year. Don't know why. They're common enough." Mr. Hobbs looked disappointed.

"Will you hand me the glasses a minute?" said Mr. Hobbs, fighting to keep the tension out of his voice. Now it was his turn to study a tree off to the left. "See that tree dead ahead? Well, there's a big limb that branches off to the right about ten feet above the ground." He handed the glasses back to Mr. Turner. "Follow it to extreme tip. There's a *bird* there." His voice broke slightly like a choir boy's.

"Barn swallows. Three of them," said Mr. Turner, scarcely touching the glasses to his eyes. He resumed his swinging stride down the wagon track. There was a long silence.

Mr. Turner appeared to be brooding. "I nearly missed that

thin-shinned hawk," he said. "This has been a bad season for me even though I *have* spotted more birds than I ever have before at this time of year."

"How many did you say you'd spotted?" asked Mr. Hobbs, feeling that a little interest was called for.

"Two hundred and forty-four," said Mr. Turner. "That's what I was telling you last night. And now that red-eyed vireo makes it two hundred and forty-five. I ought to see a hundred and ten or fifteen more before the end of the year. That won't be a bad score. It's the ones you *miss* that get you though. I've had two inexcusable misses this year and it worries me."

"I know," said Mr. Hobbs understandingly.

"One was in June," said Mr. Turner. "About the second week in June I should say. I was walking through country just about like this and I flushed up something in a field just behind my left shoulder. I turned fast enough. I had my eye on him all right. Then it was gone and I don't know what it was."

Mr. Hobbs turned this episode over in his mind for several minutes. "I'll be damned," he said finally.

"Not at all," said Mr. Turner sharply. "It was carelessness. Just stupid carelessness. And the second was just the same thing. I heard the note just as clearly as I hear that phoebe now—put down phoebe—"

Mr. Hobbs who had heard nothing but Mr. Turner's voice, obediently wrote down "phoebe."

"I heard it just as clearly as you and I hear that phoebe and then someone honked an automobile horn at me and I jumped aside and lost it."

"That's the way it is," said Mr. Hobbs.

"Inexcusable," said Mr. Turner.

The wagon track led past a large grove of scrub oak, twisted and contorted by the winter winds from the sea. "Ought to find something here," said Mr. Turner.

They circled the edge of the grove. A few yards ahead of them a dead tree stood beside the track. Mr. Hobbs thought he saw something move among the bare branches. He was about to call Mr. Turner's attention to it but he couldn't risk another barn swallow.

At that moment Mr. Turner's glasses shot up to his eyes and focused on the same spot. "I'll be darned!" he said. "It can't be! Yes sir, it is! It's a saw-whet owl! What do you know about that! Way down here!"

He handed Mr. Hobbs the glasses. "Well I'll be darned," said Mr. Hobbs, sweeping the glasses back and forth in a vain search for the tree. "That's something, isn't it?" He wrote down "saw-toothed owl" and they plodded on.

He was getting very tired now. They came to the southern edge of the woods. Broad fields, dotted with sheep, spread out toward the sea, gradually merging into salt marshlands. A large pond lay between the marshes and the dunes, and beyond them he could hear the muffled pounding of the sea.

Far down the shoreline he could make out the faint silhouette of Grey Gables standing on a highland above the sea. The thought of walking all the way back to it made the impulse to sit down almost irresistible.

"Well, I guess we'll have to leave the shore birds for another trip," he said.

"No sense doing that," said Mr. Turner. "Those fields up ahead are full of good stuff and that pond ought to be a gold mine."

"The only trouble is it's almost noon. It'll take us over an hour to get back and lunch is at one."

"Oh I wouldn't bother too much about lunch, old man. When you're out in the open meals are a movable feast. It's what you're doing at the minute that counts. The girls will be so busy gossiping they won't know whether it's lunch time or dinner."

Mr. Hobbs said nothing, but he had misgivings. Only last night, when they were going to bed, Mrs. Hobbs had said—whispering because of the thin walls—that if he left her alone all day with "that woman" she'd shoot him. He also remembered that her last words had been not to forget that lunch was at one.

If only Mr. Turner was a drinking man, Mr. Hobbs thought bitterly, he'd be hankering now for a nice cold martini instead of chasing through the wilderness after red-eyed pee-wees. As his mind wandered down this path his inner eye suddenly beheld a long frosted glass containing an ice-cold Tom Collins. His mouth immediately became filled with cotton.

"I'd give five dollars for a drink of *something*," he said.

Mr. Turner was down on one knee photographing the twisted limbs of a fallen oak. "Never fill yourself up with a lot of slosh when you're in the field," he said. "You feel better when you travel empty."

During the next two hours Mr. Hobbs tottered after his house guest across vast fields and oozing marshes, forcing his way through bayberry thickets and dragging his feet through loose sand.

Mr. Turner's energy seemed to increase in inverse ratio to Mr. Hobbs' flagging vitality. He wasn't satisfied with crossing the fields, but insisted on traversing them like a hound dog in search of a scent. They came at length to the edges of the pond behind the dunes. The air was alive with shore birds.

Mr. Hobbs sank down on a log. "Here's a wonderful place to watch them," he said.

"The sun's in the way," said Mr. Turner. "It's much better on the other side of the pond." On the other side they waded through tall marsh grass, kicking up clouds of mosquitoes like dust at every step. The grass grew longer as they approached the edges of the pond until it was over their heads. Mr. Hobbs began to feel like an African buffalo hunter.

Then he parted the grass on the edge of the pond and all his weariness fell from him like a cloak. Twenty feet out in the shallow water stood a bird that a man could see. Here was no formless gray blob strung on a telephone wire, no phantom sound which only Turner ears could hear, no black spot on the horizon, but a great blue-gray creature standing in transfixed dignity on one leg and gazing fixedly into space.

Putting a warning finger to his lips Mr. Hobbs pointed dramatically, much as Balboa must have pointed when, after leading his ragged Spaniards through the jungles of Panama, he first glimpsed the Pacific Ocean. Mr. Turner's camera clicked. The heron, without deigning to turn its head, flapped its great wings several times then flew slowly above the still water of the pond toward the grove of scrub oak.

"Well, well," said Mr. Turner. "So the amateur wins the Oscar. Know what that was?"

"A whooping crane," suggested Mr. Hobbs hopefully.

"No. That was a great blue heron. Congratulations."

It was almost three o'clock when they turned into the driveway of Grey Gables. Mr. Turner's knees were still bent and full of spring. Mr. Hobbs, on the other hand, had the drawn look which is characteristic of survivors.

Mrs. Hobbs and Mrs. Turner were sitting on the porch. Although they were chattering just as Mr. Turner had predicted they would be, Mr. Hobbs recognized an expression on his wife's face that he did not like.

"Hi-de-ho, you nice people," called Mr. Turner.

Mrs. Hobbs omitted salutations. "For goodness' sake, Rog—" she began, but Mrs. Turner interrupted.

"Peggy's been so upset by you boys. She thought you'd been attacked by a bird. I told her that when men go birding there's no telling when they'll get back. I kept saying to her, 'Don't worry. They'll be here when they get here.' Any luck?"

"Hobbs picked up a great blue heron," said Mr. Turner.

Mrs. Turner clapped her hands. "Wonderful!" she cried.

"Phooie!" said Mrs. Hobbs. "They're all over the place. I hope you men don't expect much to eat. We're having a big buffet supper party tonight and if anyone steps inside that kitchen he'll get shot."

19

We owe practically
everybody

The Turners, with unconscious consideration, had retired to their room to doze and criticize their host and hostess. Mr. Hobbs had also taken to his bed where he had fallen immediately into an exhausted sleep. Mrs. Hobbs had finally been left free to struggle unhindered with the preparations for her party.

For almost a month the Hobbses had been accepting invitations in the carefree spirit of those who have an unlimited time in which to repay their obligations. Mrs. Hobbs had been a well-intentioned but procrastinating hostess. Now, with the summer almost over, the enormity of their social debt had suddenly dawned on her.

Using the Turners as an excuse, she had asked everyone she could think of to a buffet supper. If they all came it was difficult to see just how she was going to feed them or even get them inside the house. At this point, however, the comfort or pleasure of her guests was a secondary consideration, if it entered into her calculations at all. Her purpose was to eliminate names from a list and if she had to jam people in like sheep in a sheepfold, why that was just too bad and their own fault for coming.

The worst had happened. The nightmare of every hostess had become reality for Mrs. Hobbs. Practically everyone that she had asked had accepted with pleasure. She had apparently been unfortunate enough to pick an off night. In an attempt to allay her fears Mr. Hobbs said that it might turn out to be a good thing. If the place was sufficiently overcrowded it would be harder for people to see what a broken-down dump it was.

And now the fateful hour was almost at hand. Outside Mr. Hobbs' bedroom the activity was that of a Walt Disney cartoon. Within, he snored softly with a calm imperturbability befitting the master of the house.

Gradually, however, the general clatter of preparation penetrated the blissful veil of sleep. Relaxed, he lay on the bed watching, through half-opened eyes, the amber yellow light of the late afternoon sun playing on the ceiling. His mind wandered drowsily over the course of his recent bird walk and recalled with pleasure its triumphant ending with his discovery of the great blue heron.

Gradually memory lapsed into fantasy. He and Mr. Turner were still bird walking, although they had now come to a strange country dotted with grotesquely twisted trees. The air was filled with the weird screams and croaks of unseen birds. Mr. Turner was writing furiously on a long pad. When Mr. Hobbs looked over his shoulder to see what he was putting down he found that it was a laundry list and that Mr. Turner was writing "12 shorts, 14 washcloths, 1 pr. underdrawers, 2 doilies—"

Suddenly Mr. Hobbs felt cold prickles in the back of his neck. While he had been watching Mr. Turner the grass around them had become very long and now reached well above their heads. Mr. Hobbs knew that something tremendous was about to happen. He pushed Mr. Turner behind him so violently that the latter fell on his back and lay quite still. "I've killed him," thought Mr. Hobbs, experiencing a deep feeling of happiness.

He crept forward alone to a place where the tall grass ended and there, standing on a rich green lawn, was a dodo bird looking just as it had years ago in the pages of *Alice in Wonderland*. A little girl with long hair and ballet slippers was standing in front of the dodo, her hands behind her back. "Put down dodo," he said over his shoulder, forgetting that Mr. Turner was dead. From somewhere in the distance came the sound of knocking.

"Come in," said Mr. Hobbs drowsily.

It was Mr. Turner, very much alive. "I hate to bother you, old man," he said "but something bad seems to have happened to the hot-water heater. Emily was in there taking a bath. She might have been scalded to death."

"Rog—will you *please* answer when I call you— For heaven's sake where is all that steam coming from?" Mrs. Hobbs had appeared behind Mr. Turner.

Mr. Hobbs was fully awake now. "Steam?" he said. He knew that it wasn't a very bright thing to say, but it was all he could think of at the moment.

"Yes, *steam*," said Mrs. Hobbs. "I do wish you'd take *some* responsibility. I can't do this whole show single-handed."

"Emily was taking a bath," said Mr. Turner severely.

"And all of a sudden," said Mrs. Turner who, wrapped in an elaborate dressing gown, had crowded past Mr. Turner and Mrs. Hobbs, "the hot-water heater gave a frightful hissing sound and something blew off the top of it like a *cannon ball*. The next minute the whole room was filled with steam. All I can say is it's lucky there was no one in the hall at the time."

Mr. Hobbs wished Mrs. Hobbs would wear dressing gowns like that.

"Emily might have been scalded," said Mr. Turner looking at Mr. Hobbs reprovingly.

Mr. Hobbs rose from the bed and followed them upstairs to the bathroom where he inspected the gray metal exterior of the hot-water heater with a judicial eye. A wisp of steam came through a small valve in the top and there was a steady gurgle of water going down a drainpipe somewhere behind it

Mr. Saltonstall removed his greasy cap with the thumb and forefinger of his right hand and scratched his head thoughtfully with the remaining three fingers.

"Blew the safety all right," he said. "Like to have blowed it through the roof. Must'a had enough steam up to run a engine. Those old hot-water heaters ain't no good anyway. Every year I try to get 'em to let me put in a new one an' throw this ol' bugger into th' cove. But I don't know." Mr. Saltonstall heaved a deep sigh and climbed up on a chair to get a better look at the top of the boiler.

"Take quite a few days to get a new valve for that antique," he said finally. "Ain't been one of them on the Island for a generation."

"But what will we do till then?" wailed Mrs. Hobbs.

"Oh, you got water all right," said Mr. Saltonstall, stepping down from the chair and turning off a valve under the boiler. "All you'll be without is *hot* water."

"But what'll we do for hot water? We *must* have hot water."

"Heat a kettle," suggested Mr. Saltonstall. "Lots do."

"But I've got thirty people coming for dinner," moaned Mrs. Hobbs. Mr. Saltonstall did not answer. The idea of feeding thirty people, when one did not have to, was so crazy that he didn't even want to discuss it.

"*We* don't mind," said Mrs. Turner reassuringly. "We'll just camp out. It will be fun."

"Everything's all right with me as long as you weren't scalded to death," said Mr. Turner.

"Oh, I wasn't hurt a bit," said Mrs. Turner. "And besides

I had a good hot bath before it happened, so *that's* out of the way. I wish you could have seen me coming out of that bathroom though." She laughed coyly.

"Yes indeed," said Mr. Hobbs.

The party was in full swing. It resembled every party that had been given in Rock Harbor during the past summer. The caterer who had cooked the food was the same caterer that had cooked similar food for almost everyone there. The same maids were engaged in dispensing it to the same people that had received it on so many former occasions.

Mrs. Hobbs was aware of all these things, yet like every other hostess she cherished the illogical hope that her party might somehow be different. She hoped this particularly tonight because not only was her school friend, Mrs. Archer Gabrielson, among the honored guests, but the latter had brought her mother, the venerable and terrifying Mrs. Thornton Barstow.

If Mrs. Archer Gabrielson was the pivot around which the social life of Rock Harbor revolved, then Mrs. Thornton Barstow was the granite base on which it rested. She was the actual owner of the historic colonial house over which her daughter presided with such distinction and charm. She was the one who probably paid most of the bills. In a past generation it had been Mrs. Thornton Barstow who decided the social fate of new summer residents. Since deafness had made it increasingly difficult for her to keep abreast of the local scuttlebutt, however, she had relinquished the torch to her daughter as the next in line of succession. Quick to sense these subtle changes, the *Island Messenger* now announced on the first day of July each year that Mrs. Thornton Barstow was visiting her daughter, the popular Mrs. Archer Gabrielson, at the latter's charming home "Millstones."

There were many people at the party whom Mr. Hobbs would have preferred to sit beside other than Mrs. Thornton Barstow. In fact he would have taken another bird walk through the darkness with Mr. Turner in order to avoid it. Mrs. Hobbs had warned him, however, that if he so much as took his eye off the old bag all evening she would exterminate him when the last guest had gone.

Mrs. Thornton Barstow had reached an age and social position when she did not feel constrained to talk unless she felt like it. This was an evening when she did not feel like it. In view of the fact that she heard the loudest sounds with the greatest difficulty, her conversation with Mr. Hobbs could scarcely be described as animated.

They shared a particularly rickety card table. The other two occupants of the table, whom Mr. Hobbs could not remember ever having seen before, were engaged in one of those intimate conversations which always made him feel that if the participants were not married they should be. Mrs. Thornton Barstow picked at her food and glared around the room, occasionally nodding grimly, as if giving permission to some unseen executioner to do his duty.

"We think your island is very beautiful," said Mr. Hobbs desperately. Five minutes had passed without a word exchanged. He felt that he had to say something or rush screaming from the room.

"What's that?" asked Mrs. Thornton Barstow.

"I say, 'We think your island is very beautiful.' " Mr. Hobbs raised his voice, watching his table companions anxiously from the corner of his eye.

Mrs. Barstow adjusted her hearing device which lay somewhat poorly concealed in the upper recesses of her abundant bosom. "What say?" she inquired.

"I say, 'We think your island is very beautiful,' " shouted Mr. Hobbs.

"I don't hear very well," said Mrs. Barstow in a confidential voice.

"It doesn't matter," shouted Mr. Hobbs. "It was a silly remark." He was conscious of an expanding circle of silence around them.

"Who made a silly remark?" asked Mrs. Barstow, tuning up her hearing aid. For the first time her aged face registered animation. "My daughter, you say? Did Augustine make a silly remark? It's not the first time."

"Who's taking my name in vain?" Mrs. Archer Gabrielson craned her lovely neck around a wing chair.

"Nobody," shouted Mr. Hobbs and then to Mrs. Barstow, screaming, "I did."

"You did *what*," said Mrs. Barstow impatiently.

"I made a silly remark," shouted Mr. Hobbs.

"What for?" asked Mrs. Barstow.

The only conversation now audible came from around the edges of the room or drifted through the open windows from the porch where the less conservative members of the young drinking group had set up permanent headquarters. Mr. Hobbs felt the desperate recklessness of a trapped animal rise within him.

"Oh forget it," he shouted, placing his mouth so near the hiding place of Mrs. Barstow's amplifier that he appeared like a man calling down a dumbwaiter shaft.

Mrs. Thornton Barstow started visibly and put her hand over her chest in a gesture of alarm. The look which she gave Mr. Hobbs was an odd combination of outraged dignity and warmth. She turned to the woman across the table. "I *do* hope you've had a lovely summer," she said.

"I'll get you some ice cream," shouted Mr. Hobbs, ignoring Mrs. Hobbs' strict instructions that under no circumstances was he to get mixed up with her food department.

The card tables of Grey Gables had one common characteristic. Given the slightest impetus, their legs swayed like those of a newborn giraffe. As Mr. Hobbs rose his knee came into sharp contact with one of the legs. The table top immediately responded with a rotary motion thereby distributing half the water in the drinking glasses over its surface.

"Where are you going?" asked Mrs. Hobbs suspiciously as they met near the front door.

"I want to see if everybody's taken care of out here," said Mr. Hobbs.

"What have you done with Mrs. Barstow?"

"Oh, she's all fixed up," said Mr. Hobbs, letting the screen door slam so that he couldn't hear his wife's comment.

Mrs. Archer Gabrielson took her mother home on the stroke of ten. Their departure was like pulling a cork from a bottle. In fact if anyone had looked into the pantry at Grey Gables at almost any time from this point on he would probably have seen Mr. Hobbs doing just that.

Nobody looked, however. They were all too occupied with one another. In fact Mr. Hobbs was becoming conscious of the fact that nobody would notice if he and Mrs. Hobbs went to bed. In other words the party was on the verge of becoming a great success.

At one point he wandered through the kitchen and out the back door. A fog had rolled in from the sea. Off to the right the foghorn on Minamatick light bellowed dismally every forty seconds.

The lights from the house streamed through the windows like banners of white smoke and the noisy hilarity within seemed to imbue everything beyond the luminous beams with sinister and brooding mystery. It reminded Mr. Hobbs of a scene from "The Hound of the Baskervilles." He shivered slightly in the damp night air and rejoined his guests.

Some time later—he was not sure just when—there was a particularly noticeable commotion in the neighborhood of the front door. One of the caterer's maids approached Mr. Hobbs. Her face had the eager look of a harbinger of bad tidings. "I'm sorry, sir, but they's some people at the door that says they want to see you. They claim they're friends of yours." The note of distaste in her voice indicated that she was used to better things.

The sounds from the front door were growing louder. Gathered round it Mr. Hobbs was dismayed to find a grotesque group of male and female tramps. They were dressed in every conceivable combination of ill-fitting sea clothes—sou-westers, oilskin pants, ragged sweaters and blue jeans. The fog-soaked hair of the women clung dankly about their faces. Several were barefoot.

A big man in oilskin pants and a lifeless-looking black jersey detached himself from the group. "Hobbsy!" he roared. "You miserable old bullfrog! We're shipwrecked mariners. Hot off the yacht. Crew of H.M.S. *Melissa*, sire, seeking succor and good cheer from ever amiable and generous—"

"I'm *Mrs.* Binger," said a tall, dark woman who might have been attractive if she removed her wet hair from her eyes. "It's a perfect imposition to land on you like this when you're giving a party. But Harry insisted that you'd make him promise to drop in if we anchored in Rock Harbor and we *do* need some milk and butter—and all the stores are closed—"

"And ice," said a voice in the background. "We need tons of ice."

Mr. Hobbs had recovered himself. "Come in," he cried, trying to roar like Mr. Binger. "Come aboard. I'd never have forgiven you, Harry Binger, if you hadn't popped in." The thought of the introductions to come entered his mind, coupled with the knowledge that he could not remember any of his guests' names. "Peggy," he shouted frantically. "Peggy."

It was midnight. The damp, ragged crew of the *Melissa* were sprawled about among the invited guests. With the assurance that comes from fighting the elements with bare hands (and feet) they had pretty much taken over. One of the crew, a baby-faced girl with stringy blond hair, had a small accordian and a young man by the name of Dack or Quack or something had appointed himself Master of Ceremonies.

He stood on a chair, waving his hands for silence. "Now mates, fill up your beakers with rum and stow yourselves 'cause you're going to hear something. You're going to hear— Hey, Captain, why don't you put the good cheer an' the ice right out here on the table where we can all help ourselves. Then you won't have to be jumping up and down all the time. Alex help the Captain carry the grog on deck. And now mates you've got a treat coming. You're going to hear our most *dis*able-bodied seaman Salty Clayberry sing "Locked in the stable with the sheep." I mean "Rocked in the Cradle—" Well anyway he'll be accompanied on the push-an'-pull by the equally *able*-bodied Vivienne Grace and that's the important thing."

Everyone applauded and screamed approval. The man called Alex, accompanied by another cruiser, came bursting out of the pantry with an armful of bottles and the ice jug.

"Hold everything." Dack or Quack was on the chair again, his arms stretched above his head. "Before you hear this beautiful rendition let's all fill up our tankards and drink a health to our genial host—" He leaned down and whispered to Mrs. Binger, then straightening up, "We'll all drink chickychick to our beloved host—Rog Hobson."

"The name is Hobbs," said Mr. Hobbs, but Salty Clayberry had already started to sing.

The last guest had gone. The Hobbses and the Turners sat on the long sofa in the living room gloomily munching saltines and drinking milk. It was a bottle which Mr. Hobbs had managed to hide from the cruisers, who had disappeared noisily into the fog in their rented car, carrying with them most of his dairy supplies and all of his remaining ice.

"Well, I think they had a good time anyway," said Mrs. Hobbs timidly.

"They ought to," said Mr. Turner, "with all that *stuff* inside of them."

"I know," said Mrs. Hobbs apologetically. "These young people get going and it's hard to stop them."

"Disgusting," said Mr. Turner.

Mr. Hobbs looked at the wreckage about him, all created in honor of the Turners. His gorge rose. "I don't see anything disgusting about it," he said. "These—"

"Let's go to bed," said Mrs. Hobbs. "It's awfully late."

Two of the caterer's maids were wearily transferring the chaos from the living room to the kitchen.

"Don't you wait, ma'am. We'll clean up."

"Oh but I must. You don't know where things go."

"What difference does it make?" said Mr. Hobbs. "I want to go to bed—for three days."

The faint clinking noises from the living room and the kitchen finally ceased. The world was silent except for the

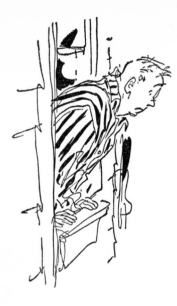

monotonous repetition of the Minamatick light foghorn, which was beginning to get on Mr. Hobbs' nerves. He found himself waiting for it with tense agony. He heard something scraping the table between the beds.

"Peggy."

"Yes."

"Are you awake?"

"Yes, I can't seem to get to sleep."

"Did you just take a sleeping pill?"

"Yes. I had to."

"How many did you take?"

"One."

"I think I'll take two."

He took the pills and composed himself on his right side, waiting for the blissful moment when the tension would relax and he would begin to sink into oblivion like a floating feather.

Somewhere outside a motor horn sounded. He paid no attention to it. Then there was a crunching of gravel as a car turned into the drive and headlights flashed across the ceiling of the bedroom.

There was a sound of voices—eager, wide-awake voices

which had not taken sleeping pills. Footsteps sounded on the porch. Somebody was knocking on the screen door.

Shaking off the drowsiness which had begun to creep over him Mr. Hobbs staggered to the window which looked out on the porch. He felt like the anonymous farmer in Paul Revere's ride. He should have had on a tasseled night cap. "What do you want?" he shouted. "The party's over."

"Hobbsy," roared a familiar voice. "We couldn't be sorrier, but we can't find the boat in the fog. We've been rowing all over the goddamn harbor since we left and our hands are all worn out—"

The speaker was joined by another shadowy figure.

"We've mislaid our yacht, Captain—"

"Keep quiet, Bert. Rog, this is Joan Binger. These crazy loons can't find the *Melissa* and we were wondering if you'd mind *too* much if we just curled up in your livingroom. We won't make a sound—"

The soft notes of an accordion floated through the window and somewhere in the darkness a muted bass voice began to sing the opening lines of "Asleep in the Deep."

20

The lull before the
storm

August was almost over.

Nature moves through the successive seasons with the irresistible force of a glacier. Its unhurried, unchanging, relentless pace is the more impressive because it is imperceptible to ordinary man. Today lies spread before him in all its beauty. Tomorrow will look the same, but that will only be because his senses are not sufficiently keen to perceive the change.

The movement of the seasons is like the minute hand of a clock which races ceaselessly toward eternity although to the normal eye it appears to be motionless. Because man can only see the changes in nature after a lapse of time has made them evident, he can never keep abreast of them. He is like a child on a Sunday afternoon walk with its parents, who is always dawdling beside the path, then running to catch up.

At the end of each August day the sun sets a few minutes earlier, but the summer visitor fails to note the difference until one evening, as he walks homeward, it is dark when he had expected it to be light.

In August the smoky sou'wester blows in from the sea, lazy, sultry, as constant as time itself. It brings with it a mysterious haze which drifts across the Island, on its way to the Mainland like a half-visible current. The summer visitor takes it in his stride if he notes it at all.

As August comes into the home stretch the wind is apt to shift during the night and one wakes to crystal-clear mornings when the dancing of the sun on the waters is hard to look at until the pupils contract and, without realizing how few such days are left, the summer visitor is torn between the instinct to rise and join this festival of beauty and the desire to pull the blankets over his face and enjoy their warmth for another half hour.

And everywhere the goldenrod splashes the land with sunshine; in meadows, along the dusty roadsides, behind the dunes, around the borders of inland ponds—unheeded herald of summer's end.

All of which leads up to the fact that Mr. Hobbs, like most off-Islanders, did not realize that the summer was almost over until the end was right around the corner. His mind continued to look forward until the last minute. Now he was obliged to wrench it into reverse and suddenly start looking backward.

Life at Grey Gables had entered a new phase. His guests were gone. The cruisers had departed on their carefree way with the lifting of the fog. Kate had returned from some mysterious visit.

Mr. Hobbs was never sure just where she was and as a result her returns always came as an agreeable surprise to him. During this last expedition she had wangled a driving license from the gullible Department of Motor Vehicles and fallen in love with a boy without a car—two events destined to have a marked effect on Mr. Hobbs' life.

Up to this point automobiles had not presented a major problem. Mr. Hobbs had his sedan, and for a period there had also been the Carvers' ancient station wagon and the Grants' equally venerable two-door. Kate's needs had been cared for by the boy with the red convertible.

Byron had driven home in the two-door, however, and shortly after the station wagon had given up the ghost. Susan said that when it got like that Stewart was the only one who could set it in motion again. So she helped Mr. Hobbs push it into the garage to await its master's return. At which point Mr. Hobbs' car had assumed the hacking for the entire family.

It was Kate, however, who had transformed the car shortage from a minor to a major crisis. Her new romance being apparently without automotive resources, it was up to her to provide transportation if the delicate roots of love were to be properly nourished.

From early morning until late at night, she was continually rushing off to unknown places which were only accessible to an automobile—and she had a passion for keeping them unknown.

"But Mother! Do I have to tell you every little place I go. I'm really not a *child* you know. I'm *not* going on wild parties. I'm *not* coming home bug-eyed and running into telegraph poles. You and Dad read too much F. Scott Fitzgerald when you were little and you've never gotten over it. It's so *humiliating*, Mother, to be cross-examined every time I ask for the car."

"Darling." Mrs. Hobbs was somewhat afraid of her youngest daughter. "You fly to pieces so. It's all right for you to take the car, but your father likes to know where it is and when it's going to be brought back."

"Why does everyone always have to talk about *Dad's* car and *Dad's* this and *Dad's* that? Is this a family or is it an oligarchy or something? All I do is ask for the car and there's a perfect scene about it. Why can't we be more integrated?"

"Where's the car?" asked Mr. Hobbs. "I told Jack Ogden I'd meet him down on West Beach and do a little fishing."

"Kate has it, dear," said Mrs. Hobbs, nervously.

"When's she coming back?"

"I don't know. They're all going to the movies at Long Beach and then they're going to the Lobster Pot for dinner. After that they're going dancing somewhere."

The veins in Mr. Hobbs' forehead stood out as he fought

for control. "Good," he said. "Good. My car goes tearing all over the Island filled with a lot of screaming maniacs dropping cigarette butts all over it—lighted cigarette butts. I can't go fishing so that a lot of children can spend somebody's hard-earned money at the Lobster Pot. Whose vacation—"

"Rog! For heaven's sake! Talk to Kate about it. Don't scold me."

He wandered into the living room and picked up our Island Birds which Mr. Turner had left for him. Mr. Hobbs was a conscientious man whether the matter had to do with birds or business. If Mr. Turner had given him a valuable bird book he felt that the least he could do was to go bird walking with it. He might even see another great blue heron. Who knew?

He took his binoculars from the hook behind the door, stuck the book under his arm and set off down the road in the direction of West Beach. The bushes on either side were alive with birds. They were darting about in such a hysterical fashion, however, that he was not able to get a good look at them. Mr. Hobbs decided there must be some kind of a crisis going on in their lives. It didn't seem like just the time to pry into their private affairs. He tried walking with his knees bent the way Mr. Turner had recommended, but it hurt his joints so he gave it up and resumed his natural gait.

About fifty yards down the road the telegraph wires were crowded with rows of motionless birds, the same strings of gray-black beads that he had encountered with Mr. Turner. Well, if you were going to identify birds you had to begin somewhere. He trained his glasses on the beads, but they were too far away. They still retained their round, meaningless silhouettes against the afternoon sun.

All the hunting instincts of his primitive ancestors rose within Mr. Hobbs. He would stalk his prey with the skill and cunning of a wild beast. Inch by inch he would creep up on these damnable creatures until they revealed themselves to him through the lenses of his glasses. How infinitely much more subtle this was than stalking game with a high-powered rifle.

With the binoculars glued to his eyes he began to tiptoe stealthily down the road. He lifted his foot high at each step and set it down carefully. To a casual observer he might have been Pan dancing in slow motion through a pagan grove, his pipes at his eyes rather than his lips.

There was a screeching of brakes and, as he removed the binoculars hastily, he found himself sighting along the shiny black hood of a sports roadster. The driver was leaning around the edge of the windshield.

"What the hell—" he began. Then his expression changed. "Roger Hobbs!" he cried. "Of all people! I didn't know you were within a million miles and suddenly I find you dancing in the middle of a lonely country road. How are you and for heaven's sake what are you doing?"

Mr. Hobbs pointed dramatically toward the black objects on the telephone wires. "Birds," he said.

The man looked at the birds and then back at Mr. Hobbs anxiously. "All right," he agreed. "Birds. So what?"

"I like to identify them," said Mr. Hobbs, feeling his face

getting red. "It's—it's a kind of a hobby. Gets you outdoors and all that sort of thing."

"Oh, a *bird* spotter. Well, for God's sake! You're the last person I expected to fall for that racket. How long are you going to be around?"

"Until after Labor Day."

"Well, you and your wife must drop in for a drink. I'm in a hurry now. I'm playing golf with Bill Davis. Give me a ring."

"I will," said Mr. Hobbs.

"And by the way," said the man pointing upward. "Those are barn swallows. They're wired onto the line. All AT&T lines come equipped with barn swallows. I'm telling you so you won't get run over again. Don't forget to give me a ring. We're in the book."

Mr. Hobbs replaced his fieldglasses in their leather case. His face was still burning. He walked past the rows of barn swallows with quiet dignity and without so much as an upward glance. The barn swallows were equally indifferent.

He came to a gate and, feeling the need for more privacy than the road afforded, crawled through it. A wagon track led off across the moors. He followed it, secure in the knowledge that here there would be neither birds nor people to bother him. Here was only gray-green moorland rolling toward the sea, land which through the ages had grown to resemble the sea itself. Above it, fat white clouds floated majestically across an enormous sky. He felt very much alone and suddenly peaceful.

It was soothing to walk over these gently rolling hills

where one hollow looked just like the last and each rise like the one before—soothing and at the same time mentally stimulating. His mind traveled back over the events of the last month and for the first time he was able to bring them into some focus.

It had all been so different from what he had anticipated— good, rich, satisfying, to be sure, but not in the way he had expected. He had learned much in a few brief weeks but there was still much that eluded him.

He had learned that the relationship between a parent and his matured children was something that could not be allowed to grow wild, but needed constant weeding and tending.

He had learned that age spans cannot be bridged and that one cannot be a comrade to an adult child or to a grandchild or to any other person, for that matter, who is too far removed in years. Such ties can only be based on need or respect.

He had learned how difficult it was to stop thinking of his daughters as children and to realize that they were adults, as well aware of rain as he was and much more qualified than he to decide whether or not to come indoors because of it.

He realized now that there was only one point where his life had truly touched the lives of his children. It was in the early years when they had been helpless and needed him because of it; when the need ceased their paths had diverged.

There was nothing depressing about that. Grown children no longer needed parents as such. That should be self-evident. When one tried to hold them by continuing to play the old role there was natural resistance. Parents wanted their children to develop—obviously not as children, but as mature men and women. It never seemed to occur to parents, however, that their children might want *them* to develop—not as parents, but as people.

His thoughts wandered to Kate. He supposed she'd be the next to go. Of course that was natural and what he wanted, but he suddenly realized that he wanted it with his head rather than his heart.

The trouble was that the minute they married they changed. It was hard to explain but nonetheless true. They went down the aisle as his children and when they turned away from the altar they were women and no longer belonged to him—or, indeed, to anyone else.

Damn it all, he was right back where he had started. It was hard for him to believe that a sensible man could resent the fact that his daughters had become quite capable of taking care of themselves. He was afraid it was at least half true though.

He tortured himself with this idea for a while, then discarded it and forced himself back into reality. He had reached the sea. The wheel tracks disappeared in deep sand. Passing between two great dunes he came out on West Beach, a strip of complete loneliness, deserted for the moment by even the gulls and the terns.

A fog was moving in from the ocean, its fingers already probing among the dunes. The pounding of the surf alone broke the silence. It was an ideal setting for the first chapter of a murder mystery. Mr. Hobbs turned and started back rapidly along the track.

He could not outwalk the fog, however. It overtook him and spread across the moors. Their friendly gray-green color disappeared and they suddenly turned dark and hostile.

He came to a fork in the wagon track. On the way in he had noticed nothing of this kind and now he had no way of knowing which direction to take. The right-hand track looked a bit more used so he followed it but without conviction. A hundred yards further on he came to a second fork. Blindly and without reason he again took the right-hand track. He was trapped—imprisoned in mist. A man might wander on these moors until he dropped, exhausted.

He thought of Grey Gables. They would all be sitting around the living room, Susan and Jane and Mrs. Hobbs, chattering in that idle, endless way which all women seem to enjoy so much. Peewee and Peter would have shaken all the toys out of the big woodbasket onto the living room floor—the unbroken, half-broken and totally demolished—thus creating that atmosphere of chaos which was their special delight.

"I wonder where Pops is," Susan might ask as it grew darker. Somehow or other he knew that she would be the one to bring it up. Now, in his hour of crisis, he felt tenderly grateful to her for it.

"Oh, he's wandering around somewhere," Jane would reply. "He'll be along."

Little did they know that at that very moment their father was staggering blindly over the fog-shrouded moors, using his last strength in a desperate effort to reach them. Eventually they would find him, of course, face downward (Mr. Hobbs was always found face downward) on the gray-green turf. His eyes filled with tears as he thought of the anguish that would be theirs.

The fog was rolling past him now in great billows, giving the whole scene a sulphurous, underworld look. From a clump of low bushes a huge bird with a great square head and big eyes rose with a rush of wings and disappeared into the murk. Mr. Hobbs leaped back in alarm and almost fell. When he recovered himself his face was damp with perspiration. He wondered if Mr. Turner would have called it a miss had he been there.

The trail forked again. Desperately he dropped to his knees and examined the ground at the junction. It seemed to him that he could distinguish a foot mark in the soft earth of the left-hand track—a foot mark *pointing toward the sea.* He bore left and a moment later, to his astonishment, he found himself at the gate. A car rushed past on the highroad.

He leaned on the gate savoring his relief. "Hobbs wins through again. Hopelessly lost yesterday in an impenetrable fog on the great moors our well-known and popular summer resident, Roger Hobbs, scouted his way back to civilization using all the tricks of the early indians who formerly inhabited this country. When interviewed by newsmen, Mr. Hobbs tended to make light of his feat. 'Anyone could have done it,' he said. 'It was just a matter of keeping cool and using my five senses as they were intended to be used!'"

"There's Pops now," said Jane, as his footstep sounded on the porch.

"Well, I've had quite an adventure," said Mr. Hobbs,

striving not to be dramatic. He hung up his fieldglasses behind the door. "I was out on the moors and the fog—"

"That's nice, dear," said Mrs. Hobbs. "And before you sit
down will you start the pump. The water hardly runs in the
upstairs bathtub, and if I don't get a bath tonight I don't know
when I ever will with all these babies and everything."

It was the end of the summer. Labor Day, that curious holi-
day which is the grand finale to all holidays, was almost at
hand. Already, anxious housewives were making reservations
for this and that delicacy at the food shops of Rock Harbor.
Swordfish had risen ten cents a pound overnight.

Mr. Hobbs had an uncomfortable feeling that somewhere
along the line he had allowed his morale to slip badly. All the
things that he had planned to accomplish remained largely
undone. The books that he had looked forward to reading
faced him reproachfully on the living-room table. Somehow
there had been no time for the deep-sea fishing trips, no time
for the vigorous routine of daily exercise that was to have
restored the tone to his less than bulging muscles—no time—
no time.

As he looked back on it now he realized that since the
first week his rate of deterioration had been accelerating. He
had long since lost his pride in having the chores done by
ten o'clock. He no longer rose at seven and descended the
path to the cove, exulting in the early-morning sharpness
as he plunged into the sea. In fact his tendency now was to
sleep later and later and even these extra hours didn't seem to
suffice. After lunch he was apt to be overcome with drowsi-

ness and on more than one occasion visitors had discovered him sound asleep on the porch swing with a magazine over his face.

Days had a tendency to resemble other days. Routines were being established. Ruts were being dug. Time was beginning to accelerate.

It was the moment of stillness before the storm.

21

The climax

Susan finished reading her letter, folded it carefully and re-placed it in its envelope. "Stew arrives Friday night, Labor Day week end, on the late boat," she said. "He's bringing Jack Halstead with him."

"Jack who?" asked Mr. Hobbs.

"Oh Pops, you wouldn't know him. He's a friend of ours that we used to see a lot of when he lived in Los Alamos. His wife died a little while ago. It's very sad. Stew ran into him in New York. He's bringing him along to cheer him up."

"Don't forget that Byron gets here on the eight o'clock boat that same night," said Jane.

"That's all right," said Mrs. Hobbs. "I have it all down on a piece of paper just when everybody gets here. I had a postal card from Kate today. She *thinks* she can make the five o'clock boat, but she can't be sure. Then Byron gets in at eight. And now you say Stew will be in on the eleven-thirty with this Mr. Halsey."

"Halstead, Mother. Please."

"Halstead then. Your father will simply have to make a lot of trips to Long Beach that day." The telephone rang. Everybody stopped talking to count the rings.

"Four," said Susan and Jane without doing anything further about it.

"Wouldn't it be possible—" began Mr. Hobbs.

"No, dear," said Mrs. Hobbs on her way to the front hall to answer the phone. "Everything's arranged."

It was a long-distance call from Kate. The rest of the family sat silently, trying to piece the conversation together from Mrs. Hobbs' replies.

"That will be splendid, dear. Of course there's room. We'd adore having them. Of course, dear. I hope you're having a lovely time."

"If that brat turns this place into a girls' dormitory over the weekend I'll kill her," said Jane.

"She will," said Susan grimly.

Mrs. Hobbs returned to the living room. Her face was beaming. "Isn't that nice," she said. "Kate's bringing three college friends."

"Three!" cried Jane.

"My God, Mother!" Susan slumped back in her chair.

"Where in the world does she think they're going to sleep?" asked Mr. Hobbs. "Listen, Peggy, that child is completely irresponsible. Do you realize that would mean eleven people and three babies in this house over the entire Labor Day weekend? I won't have it, I tell you. It's idiotic. You just go right back to that phone—"

"You're absolutely right, Pops. What does that kid think—"

"I'll tell you one thing, Mother. I'm not going to have Peewee and Peter pushed around and thrown off their feed by a lot of hysterical—"

"You just go right back to that phone, Peggy—"

"Will you *listen*," screamed Mrs. Hobbs frantically. "Kate's hung up. She's left wherever she was and I don't know where she's going. If you'll stop yelling I've got it all worked out. It's not going to inconvenience a soul. We can set up a cot in Kate's little room for one of the girls. It'll be crowded, but who cares for three nights. Then Jane, you and Byron can take the baby in with you just for the weekend—"

"I knew it. Byron and I don't get any sleep for three nights just so dear little—"

"And then," continued Mrs. Hobbs, unperturbed, "Peter and Peewee can stay just where they are—"

"Oh Mother, you *know* how Stew and I would adore to have them in with us. Then maybe Kate could ask—"

"—and the other two girls can sleep in little Byron's room. And Mr. Halstead—let's see—"

"Byron and I would be delighted to take him in with us, Mother."

"I guess Mr. Halstead will have to sleep on the sofa in

the living room," said Mrs. Hobbs. "And there you are." She beamed as one who has settled a difficult problem to everybody's complete satisfaction.

There was a brief silence. "Nuts," said Mr. Hobbs but he knew he was beaten. He strolled casually into the kitchen so that his defeat might not be too obvious.

All Friday afternoon and evening, all day Saturday, the *Island Queen* scooped its human freight from the Mainland and poured it onto the Island, like a dredging operation. In Long Beach the sidewalks were crowded with couples in bathing suits, young girls in sun suits, whole families in play suits—sauntering idly, all undressed and no place to go.

It was almost impossible to squeeze into the souvenir shops. The merry-go-round was operating on two eight-hour shifts. The shooting galleries popped and tinkled. The bowling alley rumbled and exploded woodily. In the lobster houses every table was taken and the air was heavy with the fragrance of hot melted butter. And on the long porches of the hotels the rocking chairs teetered back and forth, back and forth, back and forth, from right after breakfast till midnight.

In Rock Harbor, Main Street was so jammed with automobiles that movement had virtually ceased and one had to go outside the town to find a parking place. Harassed housewives rushed from store to store pleading in vain for someone to wait on them. Shouted sounds of greeting were in the air.

As the day wore on the focus of activity was transferred from Main Street to the charming, elm-shaded lanes which branched from it like the veins of a leaf—crooked lanes, bordered by white colonial houses between which one caught glimpses of green lawns and gardens.

From half past four on, the lawns were apt to be covered with people—people with a glass in one hand and a sandwich in the other, chattering eagerly with people whom they had seen at similar parties all summer and whom they were about to see frequently at similar parties during the next two days.

It was Labor Day weekend. The end of the season. The last chance for dozens of summer colonists to repay dozens of summer colonists for dozens of martinis (very dry) and bourbons on the rocks and Scotch and sodas. The last frantic chance to slip cucumber sandwiches (very thin) and lobster salad into the mouths of those who had slipped cucumber sandwiches (very soggy) and lobster salad into theirs.

It was a gala weekend for all except the lobsters for whom it was a dismal massacre.

Further down the shore at Grey Gables things were in an unusually advanced state of chaos. Its varied activities moved at different levels, like clouds.

At the lowest level Mrs. Hobbs darted ceaselessly and untiringly, her energies fed by hidden forces, trying to run a small hotel without sufficient bedding, chairs, glasses, silverware or kitchen utensils; improvising, stretching, cheating, preparing snack meals for children, preparing snack meals for adults, making beds, going to cocktail parties, washing dishes, putting them away, getting them out again, sweeping, and in stolen moments packing everything possible into trunks and suitcases in preparation for the exodus on Wednesday.

At another level the Carvers and the Grants, although

basically anxious to be helpful, were absorbed in the unending problems of their immediate families. Yet in spite of their
absorption one sensed a tense alertness. Susan and Jane were
like boxers sparring for an opening. This was because both
of them had accepted at least ten invitations for the next
three days. They knew that someone was going to be stuck
with the job of baby sitting and neither had any intention of
being trapped or put upon although each of them had every
intent of trapping or putting upon the first unwary person who
showed weakness.

At the level above, the very young sensed the excitement
in the air although to them it meant neither parties nor
chores, but rather bottles that were not quite warm enough,
food forced between their smeared lips by impatient hands,
familiar, beloved stories read so fast that they could no longer
understand them, bedtime half an hour earlier and, what was
most confusing of all, a shift in the focus of attention which
left them, unaccountably, on its half-darkened edges.

All of these things they were prepared to combat with every
weapon at their command—and their arsenal was better
stocked than they realized.

Up among the lighter clouds Kate and her friends moved
more freely and with less continuity of direction. They had
dumped their ill-packed suitcases in whatever corner had been
assigned to them and there they now lay, lids open and contents exposed in a jumbled mound of color. They never unpacked. Whatever they pulled from the suitcases was sown
like seed over the premises. The living room, the hall, the
stair rail, even the porch was strewn with their surplus gear.

Mr. Hobbs had no idea where they were at any time, but

they came screaming back to the house periodically for a change of costume. At these moments, no matter how hopelessly their possessions were scattered about or scrambled together they always seemed able to lay their hands on just what they wanted and in an incredibly short time they emerged, not a shapeless mass of wrinkles as one might have had a right to expect, but as fresh and pressed as if they had just walked out of the cleaner's.

Then they were off again, their excited chatter punctuated by peals of hysterical laughter, as they went tearing out of the drive.

At the very highest level of all, where the air was thin, Mr. Hobbs drifted wispily and aimlessly, surveying with distaste the confusion which surrounded him wherever he turned. He picked up an old copy of the *Saturday Evening Post* and cleared his favorite chair of sweaters, bathing suits, damp towels and what appeared to be Mr. Halstead's underwear. He hated short stories, but there was no use starting a book now. He wouldn't even have time to finish a short story. Too late to start. Too late to finish.

He couldn't find anything that interested him and wandered to the rear of the house.

Beside the kitchen door a new mountain of cartons had accumulated. He carried them down to the burning place and sat down on a rock to watch the flames. A cockeyed thing, vacations. In order to have his family about him he had to spend his time dragging cartons all over the place and burning them up. For the same reason Mrs. Hobbs must spend hers stewing around in the kitchen. Susan and Jane spent theirs washing diapers, cooking children's meals, getting them up and putting them to bed. The only ones who had a real vacation were the children, who obviously did not need one.

Mrs. Hobbs raised the screen in one of the second-story windows and stuck her head out. "Roger," she called, "where in the world are you going?"

Mr. Hobbs, his casting rod over his shoulder, turned uncomfortably in the direction of her voice. "I thought I'd try the beach just once more," he said. "I guess there won't be much time tomorrow. You might call it a last fling." It was a weak joke and he regretted having made it.

"You're not going *fishing?*"

"Why not?" asked Mr. Hobbs. "There's nothing to do around here. I can't even find a place to sit down."

"Nothing to *do!*" Mrs. Hobbs voice was incredulous.

"Do you *want* me to do something?" asked Mr. Hobbs.

Mrs. Hobbs regarded him in silence for several seconds. In that brief period she was studying him, not as a husband, but as an example of a strange and incomprehensible race. "No," she said. "No, go along fishing." She pulled down the screen slowly.

Mr. Hobbs shook his head and continued on his way. He just never would understand women and what they were driving at. Nor could he understand how it was they always made you feel so guilty without really saying anything.

The great stretch of beach was deserted. An offshore breeze had flattened the sea. The tiny waves broke sleepily against the shelving sands in a series of gentle "currumps." It was like the breathing of some aquatic monster. Half a mile to the right, where the curve of the beach formed a sandy point, a colony of sea gulls dozed motionless in the sun.

Mr. Hobbs slipped into his bathing trunks and made a few short casts to warm up. He stood on the sloping shelf of the beach, enjoying the gentle push of the incoming waves, the rush of receding water against the back of his legs and the movement of the sand around his bare heels.

He hoped he wouldn't snag. These shores were seeded with his lost plugs and he was working with his last one. At the next cast he didn't brake properly with his thumb and the line snarled. Backing up the beach he sat down on a log and began the long task of picking it straight again.

It was a bad snarl and it took him over half an hour to set things in order. Then, with his line neatly reeled, he approached the water's edge once more. Some distance out a flock of terns were circling and diving. There was something in the water below them but it was a long cast. Mr. Hobbs prepared for it carefully. The plug lay behind him, just touching the sand. He brought the rod over his shoulder like a whip. The plug ran out and upward. There was a sharp "ping" as the leader snapped. The released plug seemed to gain momentum and shot out toward the horizon.

Mr. Hobbs lost sight of it among the terns and reeled in his empty line slowly. He was not displeased. It was a fitting and dramatic way to end the fishing season.

"Will you give me what clothes you're not going to wear again so I can pack them?" said Mrs. Hobbs.

Mr. Hobbs stood in the doorway of his shallow closet and surveyed his wardrobe. Most of the garments hanging on the twisted wire hangers had been there since the day he unpacked them. He had given so much careful thought to his summer equipment that it was incredible he could have been so wrong.

He took down his tuxedo. Why in the world had he thought he would need a tuxedo? Or the four pairs of colored rayon-linen trousers? Or the striped blazer? Or the beautiful beach coat which had cost a fortune? Silly old fool.

He had brought the business suits "just in case." Just in case of what? His limp neckties had been hanging on a hook, largely untouched, ever since Mrs. Hobbs hung them there almost five weeks ago. He reached down to pull out the shoes. What in the world had he brought all these for? To his consternation he found that they were mildewed.

What kind of a place had he thought Grey Gables was going to be? And yet, now that he was faced with the problem of giving Mrs. Hobbs some of these useless things to pack, he found it difficult to make up his mind. There was a long weekend ahead. Everyone would be dressing up. He took various things down, then shook his head and put them back again.

"This is about all I can let you have right now," he said. He laid several neckties, his tuxedo, a knitted sweater with a hole in the elbow and a battered pair of sneakers on Mrs. Hobbs' bed.

"But what in the world are you going to do with that closetful of junk that you haven't used all summer?"

"There isn't anything there that I might not use over the weekend," said Mr. Hobbs firmly.

Mr. and Mrs. Hobbs stood on a crowded lawn talking to a group of people. It was the last of the Labor Day cocktail parties. The guests looked tired and drawn, like troops that have been forced to remain too long in action and are overdue for a rest area.

The faces around Mr. Hobbs were vaguely familiar although he had never succeeded in identifying most of them and had long since ceased to try. Mrs. Hobbs more than made up for his deficiencies. She seemed to know instinctively just who everybody was and the most complicated relationships were to her an open book.

As a result her conversation after one of these parties was apt to add to Mr. Hobbs' confusion rather than dispel it.

"That Spendgall girl," she would say, apropos of nothing in particular. "She's the one that's going to marry Jane's friend Harry Cramer."

"What Spendgall girl?" asked Mr. Hobbs.

"You know. The pretty little two-toned blonde in the gypsy costume."

"I didn't notice her," said Mr. Hobbs.

"*Darling*, you were pouring your heart out to her for half an hour. She's staying with the Randolphs. She's Mrs. Randolph's stepniece."

"Who are the Randolphs?"

"Dear, don't *try* to be stupid. They're the people who gave the party."

"Oh for heaven's sake." Mr. Hobbs' voice would indicate that his wife had stumbled on something both unusual and interesting.

"You ought to remember the Randolphs. Marion Randolph is Emily Grosbeck's best friend."

"Emily who?"

And so it went.

But tonight they were silent as they drove toward Grey Gables along the Cliff Road.

"I'm almost dead," said Mrs. Hobbs finally.

"Me too," said Mr. Hobbs. "I think I'll have a glass of milk when we get home and then read in bed."

"I'm certainly too tired to get up a meal," said Mrs. Hobbs. "Everybody's out anyway except the babies and poor Jane."

"I ate a full meal of sandwiches at the Churchills'."

"Randolphs', darling, not Churchills'."

Mrs. Hobbs settled back with her head against the seat cushion. "It's been a nice vacation," she said, looking out dreamily over the moors and across the sea to the crimson cloud bank which sheathed the setting sun.

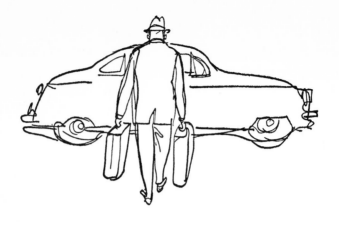

22

Off island

Mr. Hobbs' car stood in the driveway in front of Grey Gables, jammed to the roof with suitcases, cartons and paper packages. The Carvers and the Grants had pulled out the day before. Kate and her friends had left in search of new pleasures. Mr. Hobbs was not sure *what* had happened to Mr. Halstead. He had just disappeared in the confusion. And now, in a few minutes, the front door of Grey Gables would be shut and the old house would return to the dark, brooding silence from which it had been aroused five weeks before.

Mr. Hobbs had been up since dawn. He had begun the day with a final plunge into the waters of the cove. It was cold. There was no warmth in the sun as it rose in a great red ball above the bayberry bushes and there was a bite in the air which spoke of fall rather than summer.

It took courage to throw himself into the chilly water, yet, even as his flesh shrank from the shock, he was depressed by the realization that it was the last time this would be so—the last time he would struggle, on the way to the cove, with his enemy, the pump—the last time he would balance uncomfortably on the barnacle-covered rocks trying to wash off the sand before putting on his sneakers—the last time he would feel the sharp edges of clam shells scrunch beneath his feet.

It was curious how one became sentimental about the *in*conveniences of life—never about the conveniences. No one had ever gone into a tailspin about turning off an electric light for the last time or rinsing a razor under the hot-water faucet or defrosting an icebox. Mr. Hobbs dried himself slowly as he pondered this important matter. The sea gull, who had been watching him, concluded that the daily nuisance was over and returned to his rock.

At six o'clock in the morning Mr. Hobbs felt quite relaxed about the ten o'clock boat. In four hours one could do almost anything with time to spare. The packing was all out of the way. Most of the stuff had even been stowed in the car the night before. There was nothing to do but eat a leisurely breakfast, finish loading, empty the garbage, fill in the pit, burn the trash, turn off the bottled gas and motor quietly to Long Beach and the ferry.

It was nearly half past seven by the time they had eaten and cleaned up the breakfast dishes. Two hours and a half with practically nothing to do. He sat down on the top step of the porch and lit a cigarette. The pressure would be removed from life if people would only plan ahead a little. He sighed a relaxed contented sigh.

At seven forty-five Mrs. Hobbs began to produce a stream of miserable little objects which, for some reason or other, had not been packed and must now be carried loose. Other things had to be done up and there was no string. Then he had to unload most of the car to get at the picnic basket.

Mr. Hobbs glanced at his watch. It was thirty-two minutes past eight. A nightmare thought crossed his mind and he pulled out his ferry reservation to verify it. All cars for the ten o'clock ferry must be in line at nine forty-five. Scattered about him on the brown grass was a motley assortment of packages, double boilers, electric toasters, salad bowls and meaningless objects—it looked as if someone had taken a kitchen and tipped it out on the front lawn.

"Hey," he shouted. "Hey. Do you know what time it is?"

No one answered. With exaggerated calmness he walked around to the back of the house and stuck his head through the kitchen door. "We leave," he said, "in exactly fifty-five minutes."

"Well, I can't do it," said Mrs. Hobbs, "and if you haven't got anything better to do than stand around being difficult come in and get to work."

"I'm packing the car," said Mr. Hobbs and returned hastily to his post. Each to his own task. He began to fit the kitchen utensils into the spaces between the cartons.

It was twenty-five minutes before ten. No longer was it a question of arriving at the ferry fifteen minutes before departure. If they made it at all they were lucky. Mr. Hobbs had reserved space for his car a month ago. If he missed the boat now heaven alone knew how long he would have to stay on the Island. For the Summer Colonists, who had fought so hard, a few weeks ago, to leave the Mainland, were now struggling with equal determination to return to it.

Mr. Hobbs sat in the car, tapping the wheel with nervous fingers. His shirt was soaked with sweat, his hair was in his eyes and there were dirt streaks on his face. Mrs. Hobbs finally appeared, her arms full of loose objects. He hardly knew her in her city clothes.

"Oh dear," she moaned. "I know I've forgotten something. I hate so to be hurried."

Mr. Hobbs glanced at his wrist watch and at that precise moment a dark green convertible turned into the driveway. Its top was down, Mrs. Archer Gabrielson sat immaculately behind the wheel and beside her, equally immaculate, rode Mr. Kenneth Wainwright. The convertible swept around the circle and drew up beside them.

"My dears, how lucky! Another minute and you'd have been gone. Ken and I are on our way over to Bentley Farms to look at a dog and we just wanted to say good-by. We *do* hope you loved the Island and that you'll want to come back another year. Don't we, Ken?"

"We sure do," said Mr. Wainwright, carefully adjusting a light yellow muffler which he wore under his sports coat. "Now maybe there's something we can do for you. Everybody forgets something when they leave the Island. Now what have you forgotten?"

Mrs. Hobbs clapped an agitated hand over her mouth. "My God!" she gasped. "The garbage!"

Mr. Kenneth Wainwright looked startled, but showed no other signs of flinching. "Charmed," he said. "Where does it go?"

"Oh please, no," cried Mrs. Hobbs. "I'm so embarrassed. I don't know why I spoke about it. You asked what I'd forgotten and it just popped into my mind and out of my mouth."

"Nonsense," said Mr. Wainwright. "I'm the scavenger of forgotten things. What does one do with garbage at Grey Gables?"

"It's an imposition, Ken," said Mr. Hobbs, doubtfully.

"It's a pleasure, my friend. Just say where."

Mr. Hobbs glanced again at his watch. Fifteen minutes to make the ferry. "Just follow the path from the kitchen door to the edge of the bluff. The pit is right below the edge. I'll never forget it, Ken. Oh yes—and while you're at it would you mind throwing a few shovelfuls of earth over it?"

"Of course. Don't worry. Good-by. Good luck."

They started. Mrs. Hobbs made a sound, half moan, half scream. Mr. Hobbs slammed on the brakes. "The icebox," she said. "We forgot to defrost it."

"Forget it," said Mrs. Archer Gabrielson. "The firm of Gabrielson and Wainwright move into your house and take care of everything—garbage, icebox, trash, papers—anything."

"Good Lord, Ken, I forgot to empty the scrap baskets. The incinerator is right by the pumphouse."

"O.K., Rog. Good-by now. You'll miss the boat."

They were turning into the main road. Mrs. Hobbs suddenly stuck her head out of the window. "The empty bottles," she screamed.

The southwest wind, blowing strong from the sea, caught her words and tossed them back at her. Mrs. Gabrielson, standing beside her green convertible, waved a lemon-colored glove, "Good-by, Peggy. Good luck."

"Bottles," screamed Mrs. Hobbs and collapsed into her seat as a clump of bushes cut off her view of Mrs. Archer Gabrielson, Grey Gables and the sea.

They drove silently westward over rolling New England roads. Mrs. Hobbs was asleep. Her face looked drawn and her mouth, relaxed, showed lines of fatigue.

Mr. Hobbs looked at her anxiously, although his concern was not entirely unselfish. He wanted to go to sleep himself.

He straightened his shoulders and took a deep breath, fighting to throw off the drowsiness that was creeping over him like an anesthetic.

Summer was over. The day after tomorrow he'd be back at his desk. The thought made him wince. If he only had three or four days to rest after he got home. There should be a transition period between a man's vacation and his return to his job —a neutral yellow light which would give him a chance to catch his breath.

To keep awake he went back over the month that had just ended. He was surprised at how little imprint some things had left and the vividness of other scenes as they drifted across the screen of his memory.

The confusion, the moments of weariness, his failure to carry out his original plans, the times when he felt that he had blundered into a world to which he did not belong—all the petty exasperations and frustrations were already in the process of being washed out of his consciousness.

The pictures he was carrying home with him were of a different sort—the feel of wet sand under bare feet, the two-note cry of a scolding gull, the sigh and moan of the southwest wind as it poured through his bedroom window, the dive of a tern, the lift and fall of seaweed as the incoming tide crept between the rocks, the muted sound of distant surf, wind-blown dune grass tracing its signature in the loose, dry sand.

He saw again the nearness and immensity of the August night sky and the gray wall of a fogbank creeping in from the sea. He felt the coolness of quiet, green water and the freshness of the morning breeze on his face.

So many little things—things which one hardly noticed at the time—the smell of bayberry—a patch of goldenrod beside the road—fat, white clouds in a summer sky.

These were the pictures he was bringing home—and in the background of all of them were Byron and Peewee and Peter—fat little legs running or staggering across the sand—the sound of their laughter—trusting hands slipped into his. He lived again in what he now recognized was an atmosphere of life and vitality, yet only a few days ago he had thought of it in his blindness as hopeless confusion.

The fact that they were now all scattered again hit him suddenly like a blow. He felt old and lonely. He tried to recall some of the things they had said, but children's words are like dreams which fade away while we try to store them in our memory, and leave only the sound of their voices.

Come, come, Hobbs you're getting senile. He glanced at Mrs. Hobbs. She was still asleep.

One of the first things he must do when he got back to the office was to talk to Parkinson regarding the Montgomery matter. It should be all buttoned up and out of the way, but it would be just like Parkinson to have postponed action until Mr. Hobbs returned. The fellow was a hard worker, but he had no initiative.

Mr. Hobbs spent several miles being irritated with Parkinson.

He dreaded the mountain of mail that would be waiting for him, neatly sorted according to importance by Miss Gilbert. Most of it was of no consequence. Most executives' mail, for that matter, was of no consequence, but Miss Gilbert insisted that everything be answered regardless of how unimportant it might be.

She would have made it impossible for him to do anything else. Attached to each letter would be a neat carbon of her reply. "Your letter of August 17th addressed to Mr. Roger Hobbs has been received during his absence from the office. He will return immediately after Labor Day at which time your letter will be referred to him."

By means of this wording Miss Gilbert managed to convey the idea that if the writer did not receive a reply from Mr. Hobbs within a few days after his return it would be obvious whose fault it was—and it wouldn't be Miss Gilbert's.

And why "immediately" after Labor Day? What business was it of Miss Gilbert if he didn't get home until Thanksgiving? But she knew he would. That was the trouble.

He spent several miles feeling frustrated about Miss Gilbert.

Before he got all tangled up with that stack of mail, though, he must get hold of Charlie Speeden and Ray Harris and work out some kind of a fall program. Last year they didn't get started till November. Everybody procrastinated so. You had to keep putting ginger under their tails all the while.

For several miles he put ginger under the tails of procrastinators.

Mrs. Hobbs opened her eyes. "I've been asleep," she said.

"I know," said Mr. Hobbs.

"Don't you want me to drive a while?"

"No thanks. I'm fine."

"But you're tired. Why don't you try to catch a little nap?"

"I never felt more awake in my life," said Mr. Hobbs.

They drove for a long time in silence.

"You know," said Mrs. Hobbs, "there's one thing I'd change at Grey Gables. If there was only a tiny little separate house— a guest house sort of a place—you know what I mean—just a bedroom and a bath—overlooking the cove. Then you and I could live there and be off by ourselves when we wanted and the girls wouldn't have to have the babies sleeping in the same room with them half the time."

"That's not a bad idea," said Mr. Hobbs.

"We might even have a little kitchenette where we could get our own breakfast."

"And a flagstone terrace sheltered from the wind—"

"—and a sun deck."

"The people that own the place would never go to all that expense though."

"Maybe they'd let us build it and take it out of the rent or something."

"That's a thought," said Mr. Hobbs. "I might suggest it to them."

They were silent for several miles, each adding personal features to the little house.

"It was such a lovely spot," said Mrs. Hobbs.

"Hard to beat," said Mr. Hobbs.

23

The show is over

The wind had swung strongly into the southeast, piling the waves against the deserted beaches.

They were no longer friendly waves on the crests of which one might coast to the shore in a welter of sun-flecked foam, but sullen, sand-saturated rollers which came at the beach from many angles, jostling one another angrily as they rose and broke.

A group of gulls sat on the ridgepole of Grey Gables, facing the wind, their heads sunk against the gusts. Occasionally one would take off, circle once or twice over the little cove and return to his position.

On the stone wall above the garbage pit four crows sat motionless, watching the pit with unblinking eyes, waiting for the man in the colored shirt who used to bring them such delightful things each day.

In Rock Harbor, Main Street was almost deserted. It was the noon hour. Down by the padlocked Yacht Club, in Avery's diner, a few men sat hunched on the high stools, idly stirring coffee.

"What you going to do this winter, Joe?"

"I'm going off-Island again. I got my old winter job back in Harborport. What are you going to do?"

"Haven't made up my mind yet. Alton Raintree wants me to work for him. Guess I probably will." The sliding door of the diner was pushed back. "Hi, Chief. How does it feel not having your feet run over by convertibles?"

Mr. Peabody swung his heavy body onto a stool. "Feels good," he said. "Kind of a letdown though. Get so you miss the excitement."

"Yeah, you sure do." Mr. Avery set a cup of coffee in front of the Chief of Police. "They was running in here day an' night. Always hungry. An' yakity yakity yak. I never saw kids could make so much noise in my life. Yakity yakity yak. More coffee, Joe?"

"Yeah, half a cup. Going to keep this place open all winter, Allen?"

"Pretty much, I guess. I may do a little scalloping by 'n by. If I do Edith'll run it for me. Come January an' February we may hop in the car an' go down south somewheres. Can't tell yet. We did pretty good this year, though."

"Guess everybody did. Brent Williams was saying the Ocean House did the best business they ever done."

"Yeah, I guess that's right. What's this I hear about Brent running for selectman?"

"Somebody told me that too. Brent's a good man."

"Yeah, he's a good man, but I'd like to see Doc Easton get it."

"Well, the Doc's all right only I don't see what a sawbones knows about running the finances of a place like this. You need a businessman on that job."

"You may be right. I got to go back to work. Let's get together some evening, Allen."

"Like to."

"O.K. I'll give you a ring."

"O.K."

Peace began to settle over the Island like a soft blanket—the peace that comes when a routine has been established which only changes with the requirements of the seasons—a peace which deepens as contact with the outside world becomes less frequent and time creeps with the sun, acquiring, thereby, depth and value instead of rushing past unheeded as it does in cities.

And over the villages of the Island and their white-spired churches, over the woodlands and the farms and the moors, over the lonely, rustling dunes and the cold offshore waters, the seagulls circled—completely indifferent to the comings and goings of men.